PINE ISLAND HOME

ALSO BY POLLY HORVATH

An Occasional Cow
(Pictures by Gioia Fiammenghi)

No More Cornflakes

The Happy Yellow Car

When the Circus Came to Town

The Trolls

Everything on a Waffle

The Canning Season

The Vacation

The Pepins and Their Problems
(Pictures by Marylin Hafner)

The Corps of the Bare-Boned Plane

My One Hundred Adventures

Northward to the Moon

Mr. and Mrs. Bunny—Detectives Extraordinaire!
(Pictures by Sophie Blackall)

One Year in Coal Harbor

Lord and Lady Bunny—Almost Royalty!
(Pictures by Sophie Blackall)

The Night Garden

Very Rich

PINE
ISLAND
HOME

Polly Horvath

MARGARET FERGUSON BOOKS
HOLIDAY HOUSE · NEW YORK

Margaret Ferguson Books

Copyright © 2020 by Polly Horvath

All Rights Reserved

HOLIDAY HOUSE is registered in the U.S. Patent and Trademark Office.

Printed and bound in July 2020 at Maple Press, York, PA, USA.

www.holidayhouse.com

First Edition

1 3 5 7 9 10 8 6 4 2

Library of Congress Cataloging-in-Publication Data

Names: Horvath, Polly, author.

Title: Pine Island home / Polly Horvath.

Description: First edition. | New York : Holiday House, [2020]

"Margaret Ferguson Books." | Audience: Ages 9–12.

Audience: Grades 4–6. | Summary: Orphaned and alone, the four
McCready sisters, aged eight to fourteen, move to a house off the
coast of British Columbia left them by their great aunt, and get by
with the help of neighbors. | Identifiers: LCCN 2019052283

ISBN 9780823447855 (hardcover) | Subjects: CYAC: Sisters—Fiction.

Orphans—Fiction. | Eccentrics and eccentricities—Fiction.

British Columbia—Fiction. | Classification: LCC PZ7.H79224 Pin 2020

DDC [Fic]—dc23 | LC record available at https://lccn.loc.gov/2019052283

To Arnie, Emily, Rebecca, Millie, Laddie, Bo, and Murphy.
And to Keena, Zayda, Andrew, and Bonnie too.

Contents

PINE ISLAND HOME

The Letter

THE McCready sisters, Fiona, fourteen, Marlin, twelve, Natasha, ten, and Charlie, eight, were raised in a missionary family. They had been happily and safely moving from pillar to post all over the world when their parents, taking their first vacation ever, having come into a small sum of money from an aging uncle who "felt it strongly" that they had never had a honeymoon, invited them to Thailand, where he ran a small hotel. The three of them and the hotel were swept away in a tsunami. The four girls were, at the time, living in Borneo, in a small cottage far back in the jungle without benefit of internet or phone service, being seen after by a visiting church volunteer who couldn't continue to take care of them as she had other plans. So the church had a Mrs. Weatherspoon from Australia come to stay with them until someone in their family could step forward. That took a year.

Mrs. Weatherspoon sent out appeals to all the relatives she and the girls could find except for a great-aunt, Martha McCready, who lived off the coast of British Columbia.

The girls' mother, when opening Martha's annual Christmas card, called her "that peculiar woman hiding in the woods." Mrs. Weatherspoon said they would save her as a last resort. But surely someone more suitable would respond first. There were aunts and uncles in Tampa, Florida; Lansing, Michigan; Shreveport, Louisiana; and Kingsport, Tennessee. That was the lot. It took a while for the responses to Mrs. Weatherspoon's appeal to trickle in. The mail pickup and delivery in the jungle was unreliable and slow. After receiving the appeal, the relatives then had to think about it. These were their sister's or brother's children, it was true. But there were four of them. Fitting four children into an already-established household was no small matter. Some of them wrote to ask Mrs. Weatherspoon to write them if no one else had come forward. When Mrs. Weatherspoon did, they had to think about it all over again. This took time. And none of them had met the McCready children. Mr. and Mrs. McCready had become estranged from their brothers and sisters many years before when they had made what the siblings considered a "very weird choice," joining a church that none of them had heard of and of which, for some reason never explained to the girls, they all disapproved.

It was a very sad year but one made more interesting for the children by waiting to find out where they were eventually going to end up. Fiona, who felt herself in charge of keeping up with family practices, remembered her father's dictum to never shy away from the difficult subjects. Talk about them.

"Where would you most like to go?" Fiona would quiz the others at dinner.

"Tampa, I suppose," said Natasha. "We could swim in the ocean."

"Is Tampa *on* the ocean?" asked Marlin.

"It's in Florida," said Natasha.

"Not all of Florida is on the ocean," replied Marlin.

"Sharks," said Charlie, who tended to see danger everywhere.

"Not on land," said Marlin.

"I'm sure they'd make us go swimming," said Charlie. "Everyone always wants to make you go swimming even if you don't want to. They will make us take swim classes."

"Swim classes are in pools and you've already learned to swim," said Marlin. "I don't think you have anything to worry about."

"They probably make you take your swim classes in the ocean if you *live* on the ocean and we will be eaten by sharks," said Charlie morosely.

Marlin could understand why Charlie would be afraid of the ocean, given their recent tragedy. But Charlie, she thought, was afraid of the wrong thing. She should be afraid of tsunamis, not sharks. She was going to point this out but decided not to give Charlie any more cause for worry.

Mrs. Weatherspoon was always very quiet during these discussions. It pained her that the children had lost their parents and it pained her that they were left to such an uncertain fate. She would have taken them on permanently herself but she too had other plans and had to get back to Australia eventually.

"Not Lansing, Michigan, that's for sure," Natasha went on.

"Why not?" asked Charlie.

"It sounds the most boring," replied Natasha. "What's in Lansing? Nothing."

"It's the state capital," pointed out Fiona.

"You just said that to show off," said Natasha. "You don't care that it's the state capital."

"I'm just stating a fact," said Fiona. "Because I happen to know it. If you studied your geography as you're supposed to you would know it too."

Fiona was the quintessential big sister.

"Kingsport, Tennessee," said Charlie. "I think that's the best. It sounds like it's full of castles."

"Because it's got king in the name?" asked Marlin. "You will be disappointed. It will not only be boring, you won't be able to understand anything anyone says because they'll all have those thick southern accents where it sounds like people are trying to talk with a mouth full of marbles. And everyone there will be in love with Elvis Presley and probably wear big sunglasses and white jumpsuits."

"That's Graceland," said Natasha.

"Graceland isn't a city, it's the name of Elvis's house," said Marlin.

"Where is Graceland?" asked Charlie.

Fiona didn't know and after her geography comment she decided to change the subject.

"You'll understand the accents better in Tennessee than you will in Shreveport," she said. "I am stumping for Shreveport anyway despite the accents. There are bayous in Louisiana. I have always wanted to live on a bayou."

"What's a bayou?" asked Charlie.

"I don't know," admitted Fiona. "I just like the sound of it."

"It's something swampy and pelicans fly over it," said Natasha, who liked birds and knew where different ones lived. "I wouldn't mind living somewhere that had pelicans."

Mrs. Weatherspoon usually started silently weeping at this juncture. Her great fear and the one she knew the girls hadn't considered was that *no one* would want them and then what? These little hopeful discussions were like piercing arrows to her heart.

As it turned out none of those four sets of aunts and

uncles in those much-discussed destinations did. They were very sorry and regretful but even after so much consideration, and knowing no one else had stepped forward, they just didn't think they could do it.

Mrs. Weatherspoon was beside herself with anxiety as each declining letter arrived. As the end of her year with the girls approached she finally sent a letter to Martha McCready. Mrs. Weatherspoon had stayed on in the Borneo jungle, sure that at any second, someone in the girls' family would agree to take them. But the thing she feared most was now in play. She paced and shredded dinner rolls and generally lost control of herself while trying desperately to appear calm each time a regretful no arrived.

Fiona actually *was* calm. "What is going to happen to us now?" she asked after the fourth letter arrived.

"Social services," said Mrs. Weatherspoon through tears, "is (gulp, gulp, sob, sob) certainly a possibility." And she blew her nose into her ever-ready embroidered hankie.

"We still haven't heard from the peculiar great-aunt," said Marlin.

"No, dear," said Mrs. Weatherspoon, sniffling, "that's true but she's a bit old to be taking on four children. And I gather she's always been something of a hermit. I would not hang my hopes there."

"Then where can we hang our hopes?" asked Natasha.

"Again, social (sob, sob, gulp, gulp) services," Mrs.

Weatherspoon choked out. "You will not end up on the street but, oh my (attempt to stifle sobbing by putting a handkerchief to her mouth so the next part came out muffled), *social services* of all things!"

"What's wrong with social services?" asked Charlie, unable to account for the depth of Mrs. Weatherspoon's sorrow.

"I guess that means foster care," said Fiona. "Well, that's bad but not the end of the world. They'll find someone to take all four of us, won't they? They won't split us up?"

"That's just it," cried Mrs. Weatherspoon. "I have seen it too many times. I very much fear that is exactly what *will* happen. You will be split up. Perhaps placed in homes all over the United States. Hundreds of miles from each other. Scattered to the winds!"

And Mrs. Weatherspoon lost it completely, lying right on the floor and heaving with sorrow. Fiona was disenchanted. She liked Mrs. Weatherspoon. She was grateful to Mrs. Weatherspoon for all she had done for them this year. And for taking a year out of her life and familiar surroundings to care for them. But she found this total loss of self-control unseemly.

Besides, Fiona could see that her sisters were nearly wetting themselves at this grown-up display of despair and the news that they might lose each other. They had hung on to their courage and hope all through that terrible year.

It seemed the height of unfairness that after being so brave they were now being asked to face something even more terrifying. This was especially so for Fiona because she felt strongly her need to care for and keep together what was left of their family. The idea of her younger sisters, especially little Charlie, going to some strange home maybe hundreds of miles from her where she couldn't even keep an eye on them was too awful for words. She began to plan an escape into the jungle for all four of them if it came to that. Better to take their chances with the snakes and be together than face alone the sorrow and terror of the day-to-day wondering of what had become of the others.

For a week Fiona suffered such worry she couldn't eat but the following week as they got off the school bus and approached the house they found Mrs. Weatherspoon dancing up and down the porch stairs as if she'd lost her mind, and waving a piece of paper. When they got closer they saw it was a letter.

"What is it?" asked Fiona as Mrs. Weatherspoon waved it merrily in their faces. Fiona did not even dare to hope it might be the fifth anticipated reply.

"My dears, my dears, you are *saved*!" Mrs. Weatherspoon cried happily.

The children sat down right there on the steps and Mrs. Weatherspoon read their great-aunt's letter to them a full eighteen times. Fortunately, it was short.

Dear Mrs. Weatherspoon,

Thank you for informing me of my great-nieces' predicament. I will take them. Of course I will. Here is my address, my email, and phone number for the girls when they reach civilization where such services are available. Send me their flight times and I will pick them up at the airport here on Pine Island, British Columbia. I live outside St. Mary's By the Sea but they will come in at Pine Island's only airport on the north side of the island in Shoreline and I will pick them up there. I look forward to it.

Yours,

Martha McCready

"She looks *forward* to it!" intoned Mrs. Weatherspoon over and over between readings as if she could not believe their luck. This began to make Fiona feel very undesirable indeed. But she saw Mrs. Weatherspoon's point. They were not just being taken in on sufferance. Someone wanted them.

When Mrs. Weatherspoon got tired of the letter readings she leapt up and went inside to bake a coconut cake. Mrs. Weatherspoon, who weighed two hundred and fifty pounds, thought cake the proper expression of all joy. The girls thought this one of her more admirable traits and encouraged it always.

Later as the sisters lay in their beds in their large shared bedroom, Fiona said, "It was nice of her to be so happy for us."

"Happy for herself just as much, I bet. She gets to go home now too," said Marlin.

"That's not very charitable of you," said Fiona, using a phrase their mother had used a lot. She found herself talking more and more as their mother had, as if to remember her with a lexicon of idioms. "She's been here a year. Of course she's glad to go home."

"And it's been such a sad year," said Natasha. "It must have been difficult to witness. For a while I cried almost every day."

"I still cry," said Charlie.

"Yes, but you cried before Mom and Dad died," said Marlin. "It is just your nature."

"I'm not a crybaby," protested Charlie.

"No, dear," said Fiona, "you are sensitive."

"Mrs. Weatherspoon cries too," said Charlie. "She cries all the time. She cried every night when we discussed where we might end up."

"She's sensitive too," said Fiona.

"She won't cry anymore now," said Natasha. "We are saved."

"I hope that's the end of all the crying," said Marlin.

"Yes," said Fiona. "Mom always said you can look at

the world and see all the suffering or you can look at it and see all the joy. Let us be glad for this adventure in Canada. Let us take the view of joy."

"I want Mommy and Daddy back," said Charlie.

They were quiet after that. It was not fair to pretend that they didn't want this too and that Charlie hadn't only voiced what they all felt. But Fiona vowed privately to try and put a cheery face on things for the sake of the other three whenever possible. She would lead in taking the view of joy. Then they went to sleep.

For the next month when Mrs. Weatherspoon wasn't baking cakes on a tide of celebratory sugared frenzy, she was taking the Jeep on the long trek to the nearest city and having money transferred to Canada for the girls, getting Fiona a cell phone, making sure papers and passports were in order, and at home, helping Fiona pack. Mrs. Weatherspoon was staying behind to clean and close the jungle cottage before flying home herself. It was a busy time but finally with many instructions and warnings and Saran-wrapped cake slices, the children were put on the plane to begin their journey.

"Will there be pine trees?" asked Charlie. "It's called Pine Island."

"Big trees," said Natasha. "I looked up British Columbia in the school encyclopedia. Firs and Sitka spruces and pines."

"Ancient rain forests," said Marlin, who had also looked it up.

"Full of wild beasts," said Charlie. "I knew it."

"Some actually," said Natasha. "Wolves, bears, cougars."

"I doubt they'll come into town, Nat," said Fiona. "I doubt they live in St. Mary's By the Sea."

"Aunt Martha said she lives *outside* town," said Charlie.

"*Great*-Aunt Martha," said Marlin.

"That's too many words to say," said Charlie. "I'm going to just call her Aunt Martha."

"Me too," said Natasha.

"All right, me too," said Marlin.

"It will be beautiful, Charlie," said Fiona. "It will be like no place we have ever been, you wait and see. Remember how you were worried about snakes in Borneo but you were never bitten?"

"Hmmm," said Charlie, who was never so easily convinced, and opened her comic book.

It was many planes and many jet-lagged hours later that the girls arrived finally at the Shoreline airport. It was a small airport without even Jetways. The girls exited right onto the tarmac and walked inside. They had already gone through customs in Vancouver so they went straight to the baggage carousel, where their great-aunt had said she would meet them. But no one came to claim them. They looked hopefully at any old lady who walked by but no one recognized them or came forward.

"She must have been held up in traffic," said Fiona. "We will collect all our bags and sit here and wait. And call Mrs. Weatherspoon to let her know we got in okay."

"Shouldn't we wait until Aunt Martha arrives?" asked Marlin.

"No, let's call now so that when Aunt Martha comes we can just leave," said Fiona. "I can't wait to be horizontal. Trying to sleep upright on planes is always so horrible."

So Fiona called and Mrs. Weatherspoon said, "Well, my dears, I am glad you are having your happy ending. There is no branch of the church on the island but you can always write to me if you are in need of spiritual guidance. I will never consider it an imposition. Tell your aunt."

"Yes, we will," said Fiona.

"And call me if you need anything."

"Thank you for everything, Mrs. Weatherspoon."

"It's been a pleasure, dear," said Mrs. Weatherspoon, and they hung up.

After that the girls sat on chairs in the baggage area and waited an hour. They waited two. They phoned their aunt but got only an answering machine. Fiona left messages each time but none of her calls were returned.

"Fiona," said Marlin, "what are we going to do?"

"We are going to take a cab to her address," said Fiona. "I have plenty of cash. We will worry about things when we get there."

They were all exhausted by the thirty-nine hours of traveling. No one argued except the cabdriver, who said, "That's a long cab ride all the way to St. Mary's By the Sea. It's going to cost you."

Fiona waved a handful of bills in front of him and he shrugged and threw their suitcases in the back and said no more. It was coming to evening. The road was busy at first and then became much less so as it wound around the island's cliffside roads, the water stretching out below on one side and the pine forests stretching in a dense green blanket on the other.

"Pine trees," Fiona pointed out to Charlie, but Charlie had fallen asleep.

"Beautiful," said Fiona, watching two bald eagles circling, riding the thermals in spirals over the forest. "I knew it would be beautiful. Eagles, Natasha."

But Natasha had fallen asleep too.

The sun left a rosy peachy trail across the sky as it headed on its own journey to the west to make its way around the corner of the earth, bringing a new day to other people, people the girls had left behind in Borneo and beyond.

"It will be all right, Marlin," said Fiona to Marlin,

whose eyes were drooping, and then as her mother often said, "All things will be all right."

But they were not so immediately. The cabdriver finally made his way through one end of the charming little seaside village of St. Mary's By the Sea, all old clapboard shops leaning against each other, sidewalks trimmed with old-fashioned-looking streetlights and neat little hanging baskets spilling a profusion of greenery, out the other end and past the manicured little houses and lots surrounding it. Then they drove once more into the wilderness of long forested roads until finally they came to Martha McCready's farm. After Fiona had paid the driver and he had taken off, they knocked on the door of the small two-storied house with its wraparound porch and then rang the bell, but no one answered.

"I don't think anyone's here," said Marlin, stating the obvious and leaning on the door. She, like all of them, was on her last legs and almost crazy with fatigue.

"No," said Fiona, looking for the first time too stupefied to figure out what to do next.

Marlin searched about the mat and doorway and finally found a key under a flowerpot.

"Good finding," murmured Fiona tiredly, and opened the door.

The house was spic-and-span and empty. Upstairs there were four cots made up side by side in a large bedroom.

"Those must be for us," said Marlin. "At least we know we were expected."

The other bedroom was clearly their aunt's but was empty.

Downstairs there was food in the fridge and cupboards so they made a quick meal of cereal and fruit, took showers, and got into the four beds. Fiona wrote a note to Aunt Martha and left it on the kitchen table in case she came back later.

"I can't imagine what happened to her," said Fiona.

"I don't even care," mumbled Marlin. "I'm just so happy to be lying down. I'm just so happy to—" Before she could finish the sentence she had joined Charlie and Natasha, who were fast asleep.

But Fiona stayed awake, tired as she was, and thought furiously. She did not know what to do about this new twist in their fate. She could think of no good reason for their aunt to have disappeared. Fiona thought and thought and thought and then she too gave up and slept.

Aunt Martha's Neighbor

THE next morning when the girls awoke, Fiona held out the hope for a second that her aunt had come home in the night and they would find her bedroom occupied. She looked across the hall, saw the bedroom door still open, and got up to investigate. Her aunt's bed was untouched, and going about the house Fiona knew she had yet to return.

She put out cereal and milk again, feeling odd about taking her aunt's food without permission although she was sure she wouldn't mind, and the girls gathered as they came downstairs and settled on comfortable old chairs on the porch. The air smelled of pine and earth and the sea. It was a place smell like none they had experienced before. It was not jungly. It was not deserty. It was not cityish. It smelled March fresh and brisk and teeming with new pursuits the way a good blowing wind makes you feel exciting things must be coming your way. That it carries with it the invigorating energy of newness, new ventures, new plans, winds from across the world full of possibility.

"Mom did say she was peculiar," said Marlin. "Maybe this is one of the peculiar things she does. Disappears without warning."

"We could ask the neighbors," said Natasha.

"Does she have any?" asked Charlie, for all they could see was a huge fenced meadow and pine tree woods in all directions with mountains to the back of the property and beyond.

"She must have *some* neighbors," said Marlin. "We just can't see them from here. We should walk over after breakfast and knock on their doors. Maybe she told someone where she was going."

The girls put the breakfast things away, washed and dried the dishes, made the beds, and dressed. Then they headed down the road, Charlie holding Fiona's hand and looking into the forest the whole way, anticipating bears. The first thing they came to was a small cleared lot with a trailer parked on it. A screen hung half off a window, the steps to the front door were broken, there were an old refrigerator and bathtub on the front lawn.

"Maybe we should go on to the next house," said Natasha nervously as a large man with a mop of untidy white hair, wearing a dirty white undershirt and ripped pants, banged open the front screen door and glared down at them.

"WHAT!" he roared. "Who are *you*?"

"Our great-aunt lives next door," said Fiona.

"Not anymore she doesn't," said the man. "She buried herself two days ago."

At this Fiona's stomach dropped. This worst possibility had not occurred to her even though she had spent much of the night imagining so many.

"You can't bury yourself," argued Marlin rudely. She was the only one of them who got bristly and wanted to fight when confronted. "How can you?"

"My mother said she was hiding in the woods," said Natasha.

"She wasn't hiding in the woods, she just wasn't putting herself forward for gossip," said the man. "She didn't talk to folks. I lived beside her for twelve years and we hardly spoke. She doesn't—didn't like people."

"What do you mean she buried herself?" asked Fiona more politely.

"Just that. Oh, not *physically*, if that's what you mean. Her corpse didn't pick up a shovel or hoist the coffin into the hole before jumping into it."

The girls flinched at such bare description.

"She had it organized, I mean. She didn't have anyone doing it for her. Apparently, she trusted *no one*. She purchased her plot in the St. Mary's By the Sea cemetery—the stone was up five years before she was dead. Some folks said that was going too far. Morbid. That it would give them a chill to pass by their waiting gravestone every day on the way to town. But your great-aunt was never one to shirk from reality. She knew folks our age can go just like that." He snapped his fingers. "And she did. She dropped dead in the hardware store. Massive heart attack. Only sixty years old. But she was all prepared. She left no mess. She had an undertaker lined up, her will made, her affairs in order. She knew not too many folks would come to her funeral so—wait a second—is that what you're here for? No, you're not here for the funeral. I bet you didn't even know she was dead. You're the four she was expecting."

"I thought you said you never talked to her," said Marlin.

"Marlin..." said Fiona warningly.

"Well, you're too late," said the man as if Marlin hadn't spoken. "As I said, she's dead. She left me some of her old fishing gear and you all the house and everything else. She changed her will two weeks ago. If you hadn't shown up I would have gotten it all. Not that I give a fig. Hiram Pennypacker, her lame excuse for a lawyer, called yesterday to let me know. I don't think he knew about the four of you still coming here until I told him. He was trying to figure out how to find you to let you know of your inheritance. I'll be coming over to get the fishing gear out of your shed one of these days."

"Why you?" asked Marlin.

"Because the fishing gear is *now mine*," he said slowly as if Marlin were dim-witted.

"No, I mean why would she leave it to *you*?"

"Marlin..." said Fiona again.

"Well, he said he didn't know her," said Marlin. "So that's a reasonable question. Why leave everything to someone you don't know? Or even just the fishing gear? Why leave anything?"

"No one knew her," said the man. "No one knows me either. I got no time for it. I told her not to take on four kids but you could never tell her anything. She was..." Suddenly the man seemed choked up and turned around and slammed back into the trailer.

"Well," said Fiona as they all stood in shock, half expecting the man to come back out and finish his sentence, but he didn't. "I guess we got what we came for. I guess we found out why she didn't come to meet the plane."

They turned around and started to walk back to the house. At the bottom of their driveway, as if it had just occurred to her, Marlin said, "We're back to square one. Social services."

Charlie began to cry loudly and hiccup. "They're going to take us away? We won't be together anymore?"

"No," said Fiona. "No, they aren't. We have a house of our own now. We're not just renting. Aunt Martha left us everything so that probably means some money on top

21

of Mommy and Daddy's. We'll have to find out how that works. I guess we'll have to see her lawyer, Mr. Pennypacker. We'll have to get the money put in an account for us the way we did after Mommy and Daddy died. Mrs. Weatherspoon talked to Aunt Martha about the arrangements. I have it all written down somewhere. Our money from Mommy and Daddy is in the Canadian Imperial Bank of Commerce, a branch in St. Mary's By the Sea. We may be able to live fine on that for now. Maybe for a long while, until we're old enough to get jobs."

"Why don't we call Mrs. Weatherspoon and tell her what happened?" asked Natasha.

"No," said Fiona musingly. "I think as badly as she'd feel about it, that would only land us in social services again."

"Then that means we have no grown-up," said Marlin. "Aren't they going to object to that?"

But Fiona was thinking. Who was the *they* this time? The last time it had been the church but the church wasn't keeping track of them anymore, was it? They had them safely placed in a new home with a family member. Their part in things was over. If they didn't tell anyone they were living without a grown-up, who was to know? Who was to care now what became of them?

"Do we send out letters again? To all the aunts and uncles begging one of them to take us? Maybe we could offer to pay them?" Marlin said half jokingly.

Fiona was quiet for a minute. Something that had been said here had sparked an idea but she couldn't quite grasp it, reeling as she was from this impediment to their safe new life.

"Charlie," she said, "don't cry. I think there's an idea somewhere in my brain. I just have to try to shake it loose."

"What are we going to do?" asked Charlie, ignoring Fiona's admonition not to cry.

"Well, we are going to explore our new property. We are going to see what food is in the cupboards and if there's dry yeast and flour I am going to bake bread. Mom always said that she got her best ideas kneading bread. Don't you remember that's the first thing she would do when we got into a new home? Because it made the house smell like all our other homes? She said baking bread smells the same no matter where you end up."

"All right," said Charlie.

They spent the next hour walking the property. There was a small orchard in one corner of the large fenced-in meadow and other trees scattered throughout the rest of it. Way at the far end of the fenced meadow were a couple of large shelters.

"Those look like stables. She must have had horses at some point," said Natasha. "Too bad not anymore."

"I don't think we can afford horses," said Fiona. "We may have to be very careful with money. I haven't paid much attention to what we have because Mrs. Weatherspoon did that and I expected Aunt Martha to when we got here. But now I need to sort that all out. So no, for now, no horses."

They found a rocky path that took them down to a small beach. The tide was out and the water was shallow for a long way warming in the sun.

"Is this our own beach?" asked Charlie.

"I guess it is now," said Fiona.

"Well, we've never had one of *those* before," said Charlie, cheering up. "*That* doesn't cost anything."

They waded and put their fingers in sea anemones, watching their tiny tentacles closing around their fingers. They spied huge colored starfish with many arms lying among the rocks. Charlie thought they were octopi at first and cried out but Natasha explained what they were and also pointed out that the thing to stay away from was the translucent hard-to-see jellyfish that floated here and there. "They sting," she said.

By noon, feeling salt-encrusted, hair-tossed, and sun-soaked, they went up to the house, where Fiona made them lunch from the huge supply of cold cuts their aunt had clearly bought for them. Then Fiona shooed them away to read their books or make wildflower chains while she rummaged in the kitchen and found with delight that she had all the ingredients for bread. She put the yeast and water together but nothing happened the way it used to for her mother and she was puzzled. She called Marlin. Marlin looked at it, read the recipe from the internet on Aunt Martha's MacBook Air, stuck her finger in the water with the yeast, and said, "I think your water was too cold." She dumped it out. "Let me."

Fiona watched as Marlin carefully began a new batch and this time the yeast foamed as it should. Marlin then added the other ingredients and kneaded the dough over and over and over on the small wooden kitchen table. By the time Marlin had it in a bowl covered in a dish towel to rise and the kitchen cleaned up again, Fiona had found part of the idea that had been germinating in her brain and she called the others to the porch.

"As I said before, we have money, some anyway," she began. "And a house. We can go tomorrow and register in the schools. I like it here. I'm sure it's better than Lansing, Michigan, would be or Kingsport, Tennessee. And we're still together. Those are all pluses."

"I like it too," said Marlin.

"Yeah, me too," said Natasha.

"I want Mommy and Daddy," said Charlie.

They ignored this. They knew at some level Charlie still felt that if she repeated this enough she could somehow resurrect her parents with the force of sheer longing. They did not encourage this but they did not discourage it either. Fiona thought it was a sad thing to witness but it would be worse when Charlie finally stopped.

"We have everything we need. The only thing that other people think we need is a grown-up. But I think I can care for us. I don't think we *need* a grown-up."

"Doesn't matter what you think," said Marlin practically. "No one is going to let us live on our own once they find out that's what we're doing."

"That's what I wanted to talk to you about," said Fiona. "We can go on living here as long as no one *knows* we're living on our own. Aunt Martha doesn't seem to have talked to anyone. Except for that neighbor. And the lawyer, who didn't even know we were on our way here until the neighbor told him. So maybe, just maybe, nobody else even knows about us."

"They'll know about us when we show up at school," said Natasha.

"We could just not go to school," said Charlie.

"We have to go to school," said Fiona firmly. "Mom and Dad wanted us all to get a college education."

"How are we going to afford *that*?" asked Marlin.

"I don't know," said Fiona. "We'll figure that out, I hope. But in the meantime, we're not becoming a bunch of dropouts."

"Then the school *will* know about us," repeated Natasha.

"Yes, but they won't know we are on our own. Not if

we don't tell them," Fiona went on. "And that's the tricky part. We have to, and I mean *all* of us, Charlie, we have to keep our lips zipped about that. And it will be hard. It cannot slip out to anyone, not to any friends we make, not to this lawyer we will have to go see, not to teachers, not to anyone at all. Can we do that?"

"Yeah, sure," said Natasha.

"Well, I can," said Marlin. "The one I'm worried about is Charlie."

"I won't tell," said Charlie solemnly. "I can keep secrets."

"This is the most important secret you will ever have to keep, Charlie," said Fiona. "Everything and I mean *everything* depends upon it."

"What will we do if someone asks about our parents?" asked Natasha.

"I don't know. I don't have that part totally figured out. For now, just be vague. Don't make up any elaborate lies. Just try and change the subject or say something truthful about them without happening to mention that they're dead," said Fiona.

"Yeah, like that's going to work," scoffed Marlin. "I give this plan a week at most."

Charlie began to cry again.

"Crying won't do you any good, Charlie," said Marlin. "You have to toughen up about this. You have to be fierce."

"I can be fierce," said Charlie, drying her eyes.

"Okay then," said Fiona. "Plan one, enjoy the rest of the day, and tomorrow I will go with the three of you to school to get you registered and see if they want you to begin that morning and then head to my school to do the same. I have looked on Aunt Martha's computer and you all go to Greenwillow Elementary, grades kindergarten through seven, and I go to St. Mary's By the Sea Secondary, grades eight through twelve. They're across the street from each other. We probably saw them driving in but I don't remember. We were all so tired."

"How will we get there?" asked Natasha.

"Tomorrow we will have to walk and then I will sign us up for the school bus if they have one and hopefully it will pick us up not too far away from the house. One thing at a time."

The rest of the day was spent with Marlin finishing baking the bread, Natasha and Charlie exploring the haylofts over the stables, and the four of them taking the fresh bread and butter for supper down to their beach and eating it while sitting on a log watching the tide come in.

"Look," said Natasha, pointing at some angular white birds.

"Seagulls," said Charlie.

"No, arctic terns, migrating back up north," said Natasha, who had already looked up all local bird life but hadn't expected to see terns. She knew of them and knew they migrated but hadn't known they passed over Pine Island.

The birds turned from one side to the next looking like paper airplanes, their sharp lines slicing the air, the light reflecting off their brilliant wings as if they were glass.

"Arctic terns!" exclaimed Natasha, repeating the magic of their name, awed by seeing a bird she had never expected to.

That night they moved two of the cots into Aunt Martha's room so that Marlin and Fiona, who liked to stay up later reading and chatting, wouldn't disturb Charlie and Natasha once they fell asleep. As they lay there, Marlin put her book down suddenly and said, "It will never work, you know. Too much to go wrong."

"It has to work," said Fiona. "We are out of options."

"Has to and *will* are two different things," said Marlin, ever the practical one.

"I need you to believe it will, Marl," said Fiona. "I can't propel us forward on this hope all alone."

"Okay," said Marlin. She was touched by the faith her sister put into her to carry part of the weight of their decision to go it alone but privately she was thinking, *I will say I believe it will work but that's not the same as believing it any more than* has to work *and* will work *are the same.*

Fiona was thinking that she could not bear to be parted from her sisters. They each had quirks and qualities that had melded together as if all of them together were one thing. One entity. She always believed she could save the people she loved through the force of her determination. Charlie always had one eye out for danger like the family watchdog. Natasha floated through life like a poet, seeing birds and the slant of light on things, alive in the moment without any thought to what might happen next. Marlin had her feet planted fully, stubbornly on the ground. It was as if they all shared the parts of each other that were missing in themselves. There were good and bad sides to these qualities that they brought to the table but she would not change any of them from what they were. She dearly loved both the good and inconvenient aspects of their natures, and her sisters' natures had become somehow part of her own so that she did not even know who she was without the other three. She did not want to be apart from them. She feared aloneness for herself but she feared it even more for her sisters. The pain it would bring to her was terrible to contemplate but pain for them was unthinkable.

Miss Webster

BEFORE they set off, Fiona Google-mapped the walk time to school and found it would take them forty-five minutes. She hurried them out the door, figuring if they did arrive a little late it wouldn't really matter as they might only be registering, not attending classes that day anyway. They'd had lots of experience with new schools around the world and knew that each had its own ways. As they went down the road she worried that the schools would not let her register the four of them but would want a parent with them to sign things but she kept this worry to herself, cheerfully pointing out big old barns and huge trees and other points of interest.

Once at the elementary school, as they made their way through arriving children and found the school office, her hands began unconsciously to knit and unknit themselves. Marlin gave her a sharp jab with her elbow and when Fiona realized the nervous picture she was presenting, she stopped, drew herself up, and entered the school office prepared for battle.

But instead of arguments about their parentless state,

the school secretary came running up to the counter saying, "There you are. I bet you're the McCready children, aren't you? Your teachers have been told you're coming. Your great-aunt registered you last week. We thought actually we'd see you yesterday but, silly me, I forget about jet lag. All the way from Borneo, my! I've never been farther than Vancouver. I bet you needed at least a day to get yourselves in the right time zone, now, didn't you? Dear, if you're Fiona, I know your great-aunt said you'd be going to St. Mary's Secondary and that's across the street. I'll see to your sisters if you want to hustle over there."

"We were wondering about a school bus?" said Fiona.

"Well, your great-aunt said she'd be taking you both ways," said the secretary. "Or, oh gosh, I forget, she passed, didn't she? I'm so sorry. Did your family get here in time for the funeral?"

"Um, no," said Fiona, while the other three looked uncomfortable and tried not to express the panic they were feeling at their parentless state being somehow any moment found out and their hopes and plans coming to nothing.

"That's a shame but it was sudden as I recall. Well, I'll sort the school bus. No problem. You'll all be on the same one. Both schools share the two buses. There's one that goes west and one that goes east. You'll be on the westbound, which leaves from the secondary school parking lot. Most kids are on the eastbound, which leaves from our lot, so don't forget and get on that one. I'll make sure you're on the list and a stop is put in for you. It'll all be arranged by the time school is out. Just tell the driver you're the McCreadys and you'll be his last stop in case he forgets. Imagine you living way out there at Miss McCready's place on Farhill Road. She's got a lovely heritage farm. Or did have. Although, I guess she never did much farming. A fisherman, wasn't she, really? But such a beautiful old farm she bought there. They're always the loveliest, aren't they, the old ones? It used to have quite the apple orchard but I guess she doesn't do much with the apples anymore, does she? Shame."

"She doesn't do much with anything anymore," whispered Marlin to Natasha.

"As far as we know," whispered Natasha back because she'd been taught everyone went to heaven and she figured you must do *something* there. You didn't just sit around and twiddle your thumbs.

Fiona gave them both a hard look for whispering.

"Oh gosh, there I go again. On about the apples. I do love heritage apple trees. And she's got a bunch of different kinds of old fruit trees, not just apples. That's really all I know about her. She kept to herself I believe."

"At least we'll have free fruit," said Natasha, and Marlin nudged her with her elbow. The secretary didn't seem to notice as she went to her desk to put down her papers.

"Now, I'll take the three of you to your proper class-rooms. You can go now too, dear," she said to Fiona, who thanked her and ran across the street to the secondary school, where she was likewise welcomed and shown to her classroom. She was so relieved at how much easier it had all been than anticipated that she didn't even mind that she had forgotten to pack lunches. They'd be ravenous by the time school was out but that was certainly not the worst thing that could happen to them and she'd remember to pack lunches tomorrow. There was a learning curve to being in charge.

Many of the schools Fiona had gone to had had her going from classroom to classroom for different subjects. In other schools, often in out-of-the-way places, children of all ages shared a single classroom. In this school, it seemed there were enough students for one grade nine class with one teacher.

Going into the classroom the first time was always the worst moment in a new school but she found this one friendly enough. School wasn't going to be a problem, she decided. Keeping friends at arm's length so they couldn't discover the girls' situation without the McCreadys appearing unfriendly was going to be the hard part. But they could figure that out as they went along. She was hopeful again that this desperate plan might just work.

After school Fiona looked in the parking lot for her sisters and found instead the secretary from the elementary school waiting for her. She approached smiling and said,

"I think you'd better come with me if you don't mind, Fiona. We're in a bit of a quandary over in the office."

"What kind of quandary?" asked Fiona nervously.

"You'll see," said the secretary but not in a mean manner.

When they got to the office she found Charlie, Natasha, and Marlin sitting on chairs looking miserable. The principal was with them. She was younger than most of the principals Fiona had known. She was pretty with short dark hair and a friendly open face. She smiled when Fiona came in.

"Oh, hello, dear," she said. "I'm Miss Webster. The thing is that we just want to clear up what is happening with your parents. We've gotten a different story from each of the girls' teachers."

"Oh," said Fiona.

"Now, Charlie says your parents are dead..."

"They are," said Charlie.

The principal held up her hand while Marlin raised her eyebrows warningly at Fiona.

"Marlin says that they are busy. And Natasha says they are still in Borneo and will be joining you shortly. I know your great-aunt has passed away, dear, so I did want to clear this up. All we want to know is who is taking care of you at present so we know who to call if there is a problem."

Fiona looked at the principal. Then she looked at the secretary. Then she looked at the wall. She willed herself to come up with a good intricate lie that would tie her sisters' three stories together so that they made sense but her mind was like a deer in the headlights and refused to cooperate. The secretary had gone to grab her things to leave for the day and called to them cheerily as she closed the door behind her. Now it was just the five of them.

So soon. No, no, no! This can't be happening to us so soon, thought Fiona. It had occurred to her that they might eventually be found out but not on the very first day. Charlie began to cry.

"Oh, don't cry, dear," said Miss Webster. "You're not in any trouble. But someone's story must be the true one and I'd like to hear it from your sister as she's the eldest."

"Well, um, all the stories are true in a way," said Fiona, wondering if she could double-talk her way through.

"How is that, dear?" asked the principal, sitting down behind her desk and looking gently inquiring.

"Well, they're, you know how it is when you're moving and you lose things?"

"Are you saying you lost your parents?"

"No, no, *lose* is too strong a word—although in a sense, of course, yes, that is it exactly but can we ever really lose anyone, that's more to the point."

"All right. Let's stop talking gibberish," said the principal but she didn't look angry, only concerned. "Who is taking care of you at your great-aunt's house because I know it isn't your great-aunt. Also, you should know I was an inveterate liar in my day and am familiar with all the ins and outs of disguising the truth."

"No one," said Fiona flatly. "At present."

Marlin, Natasha, and Charlie looked at Fiona in dismay. Wasn't this exactly what she had told them not to admit?

"So, someone *is* coming?"

"Oh, most certainly, you would think, wouldn't you?"

"As you know, what I think is neither here nor there. But good try. I told you—inveterate liar. Marksman class," said Miss Webster. "Now tell me, why would Charlie say your parents were dead if they weren't? And if they are dead and your great-aunt is dead, who exactly is staying with you? Whom may I contact?"

"Well, me for the moment," said Fiona.

The principal said nothing. There was a long silence while she stared at the wall as if figuring something out.

"But we can take care of ourselves perfectly well," said Natasha. "Fiona said so."

"Natasha," said Marlin in alarm.

"Well, that's what she said," protested Natasha.

"So, there's no one? No guardian? No church member? I know your great-aunt said your church was sending you out here. She did *not* tell me your parents had died. Your aunt was never one to use two words when one would do but that seems a pretty big omission even for her."

"We have each other," said Natasha.

"Natasha..." said Marlin warningly. She did not think they should be improvising. She thought they should leave it to Fiona to be the spokesman. It was clear the trouble they got into when they all started telling different stories.

"No doubt, no doubt," muttered the principal.

Charlie chose that unfortunate moment to say, "I want to go home. I'm hungry!"

Miss Webster leapt on that immediately. "Have you not been fed?"

"I didn't have a lunch," said Charlie.

This time Marlin elbowed her so hard in the ribs that Charlie screamed, "OUCH!"

"I forgot to pack them!" said Fiona. "It was a mistake. It won't happen again."

There was another considering silence and then the principal sat up straight suddenly as if deciding something and said, "I'm going to have to call social services and see what they want me to do with you."

She started to reach for the phone receiver and Fiona was shocked to find her hand, as if by its own volition, clamp down on the principal's wrist so that she couldn't lift the receiver. She had never manhandled a stranger let alone an adult before. Natasha gasped. Marlin's eyes got large and Charlie squealed.

"Don't do that," Fiona begged. "Don't call social services. Please! At least wait and let me tell you the whole story."

Miss Webster let go of the phone, sat back, and waited.

With many pauses and insertions and interruptions in Fiona's story by Natasha, Charlie, and Marlin, it all came out.

"There could be nothing," Fiona summed up, "nothing worse than being split up. You can't imagine. You can't imagine what it is to suddenly lose your parents and then find that you are to lose your sisters too. I'll run away before I let it happen. I'll run away and take them with me. I'll run into the woods if I have to. I don't care what happens to us as long as it happens to us together. If you call social services we will be gone before they can get here."

"Don't threaten me," said Miss Webster. "Just sit there and let me think about this for a minute."

For the third time there was a long silence but this one was even longer than the others had been. Finally Miss Webster said, "You are wrong on one count. I do know what it is like to lose your family. I ran away when I was only a year older than you. I had an…unfortunate living situation. I ran away and I lived on the street for a long time. Then I turned things around and got an education. I was very lucky. I had a lot of help. And now I'm the youngest principal St. Mary's By the Sea has ever had." She blushed as if embarrassed by her outburst of pride, then added, "Not that St. Mary's By the Sea is very big or has had that many principals."

"No, but it's *still* an achievement!" said Natasha encouragingly as she knew her mother would have.

"Thank you," said Miss Webster, coughing. "I didn't mean to bring me into it. All right. You seem like nice girls. You are lucky that I was the first one to discover your secret. And I hope I am the last because here is what I am going to do for you and why. I know social services better and more personally than anyone in St. Mary's By the Sea might suspect so I have more sympathy for you than many would and I think you are quite right to be alarmed at the prospect of being placed in care. You *would*, as you fear, most probably be split up because keeping you together, while important, would not be their first priority. Finding homes, any homes, would be. And I agree, staying together *should* be *your* priority right now. As long as you can manage it. As long as you're up for the responsibility, Fiona, because most of it will fall to you as the eldest. I know a desperate fourteen-year-old can do a lot more than people think she can. I did a lot more than anyone gave me credit for but it's nevertheless very difficult to be on your own, more so than you yet know. I found it so and I didn't have three others to care for. On the other hand, you have things I didn't. You have a home and money in the bank. And you have a lot of experience, having lived all over the world. You might just do okay. Still, if I look the other way that makes me culpable. And also responsible for the outcome of this experiment."

"No, you needn't feel that way," said Marlin. "We won't hold you responsible."

"It has nothing to do with you. I hold me responsible," said Miss Webster. "And because of that I plan to come over once a week to inspect and make sure things are running smoothly. Is that understood?"

The four children nodded madly like a line of McCready bobble-head dolls. It almost made Miss Webster, who was feeling punchy with the enormity of what she could be facing in terms of losing her job and criminal prosecution and goodness knows what else, feel like laughing hysterically.

"And in return for keeping your secret you must keep mine. You must never tell anyone that I knew about or approved this arrangement, is that understood? If you are outed and face the worst, there's no sense people knowing that I knew as well. Do you promise?"

"Yes," said Fiona solemnly. "You have my word, all our words."

"We're so grateful," said Marlin.

"Thank you," said Natasha.

"We missed the school bus!" said Charlie, jumping up suddenly as she noticed the almost-empty parking lot.

"Never mind," said Miss Webster, rising and grabbing her purse and keys. "I'll give you a lift home. It will give me a chance to see how you're set up there and reassure myself."

Miss Webster drove them home and Fiona gave her a tour around the house.

Miss Webster noted the clean kitchen, the beds all tidily made. Then, because it was such a lovely day, they gave her a tour of the meadow, the orchard, and down the private path to their own little beach.

"This is so charming," said Miss Webster when they were done and standing by the fence looking across the property. "I've always wanted a farm like this but this one on the ocean, it's enchanting. It kind of has everything, doesn't it? I bet when your great-aunt bought it way back when, she got it for a song. I doubt I'll ever be able to afford such a place. Lucky girls. Lucky, lucky girls." Then she caught herself and added, "In some respects. All right!" She clapped her hands together as if a decision had been made. "I'm sure there will be bumps along the way and anticipating what they will be will probably keep me up nights but I guess you're good for now. The bus will pick you up tomorrow morning at eight-thirty at the end of Farhill Road. I'm going to give you my cell phone number. Phone me if you need something or get in trouble."

They walked as far as the house with her and went onto the porch, waving and thanking her again.

"Never mind that. Just don't forget to pack the lunches," she said over her shoulder, walking back to her car, and the girls heard her muttering to herself, "I'm going to regret this. I know I'm going to regret this. Stupid decision. Stupid, stupid decision."

"She's not stupid," said Charlie as they sat on the porch steps watching Miss Webster's car drive away.

"No," said Fiona musingly. "I think she's very brave."

"I think she learned to be brave living on her own at our age," said Marlin. "And now she can be when she has to be."

"Well, that was a bullet dodged. How shall we celebrate?" asked Fiona.

"Cake," said Marlin. "Mrs. Weatherspoon has apparently infected me with the need for cake on all occasions."

"We don't have any cake," said Natasha.

"No, but that doesn't have to be a permanent condition," said Marlin. "I'm going to see what Aunt Martha has in her cupboards."

"Our cupboards now," said Fiona absently.

"Right. *Our* cupboards. And make a cake from it."

"We don't have a cookbook," Natasha reminded her. She had already explored Aunt Martha's library the day before when they'd needed a bread recipe and knew that there were shelves and shelves of books but not a single cookbook.

"I'll check the internet again," said Marlin. "I can find all the recipes I need there. And that reminds me, Fiona, won't things like the internet get shut down if we or rather Aunt Martha stops paying her bills?"

"Well, she's only been dead four days," said Fiona.

"When we go into town to speak to her lawyer I think we can ask about that as well."

"Without somehow giving away that we will be paying the bills ourselves," said Marlin.

"Yes, that will be the tricky part," said Fiona, grabbing her head. "Never mind, let's get homework out of the way while Marlin makes the cake. I'd better call the lawyer's office now before I lose my nerve. I suppose we will need an appointment."

With a stomach that felt full of rocks, Fiona shut herself in Aunt Martha's office and phoned the lawyer. When Mr. Pennypacker's secretary took Fiona's name she said, "Oh!" as if surprised, as if she had heard Fiona's name before and was startled to be speaking to her in person, but then efficiently scheduled an appointment for them without further comment.

While Fiona made her call, Marlin scrounged around the kitchen finding, among other things in the cabinets, almond flour, and in the freezer, frozen cherries. So, after perusing the internet, she decided on an almond cherry cake. It was easy to make and she made it in a glass nine-by-eleven-inch pan. By the time they'd finished homework and eaten a supper of canned soup and grilled cheese, the cake was cool enough to eat.

"This is really good," said Fiona, taking a large bite.

"You're a natural cake baker," said Natasha.

"I think I am," said Marlin, who then sat down to finish her own homework while the others cleaned up the kitchen and Fiona packed lunches for the next day.

Finally, they collapsed in their beds worn out from a day full of adrenaline surges and fell asleep to the loud orchestration of the tree frogs, screaming to the others in their March frenzy to find a mate.

Miss Webster collapsed in bed too, worn out by hard decisions, but she was wrong about being kept awake worrying about things that could go wrong. She slept just fine. It was Fiona who woke up time and again worrying. For something else had occurred to her.

This isn't going to work, she thought, staring at the Big Dipper, which hung in the right-hand corner of the window, spilling a river of starlight into the inky night. *We need a grown-up to pretend to be caring for us. If we'd had that, Miss Webster would never have found out our real situation.*

On the face of it this would be a difficult find because the girls as yet knew no one. But Fiona had an idea about that too.

Al Farber

WHEN the girls got up and Natasha headed to the cake pan, deciding to make cherry and almond cake her breakfast, Fiona barked, "Don't touch that cake!"

"Even Mrs. Weatherspoon let us have cake for breakfast," protested Natasha. "She said it was no worse than donuts."

"Mrs. Weatherspoon was the size of a house," said Marlin. "Is that what you want?"

"Marlin, that's not nice," said Fiona. "And anyway, that's not why I don't want you to touch the cake. I have other more important plans for it."

"What plans?" asked Charlie.

"Never mind," said Fiona. She didn't want three versions of the plan somehow slipping out of three mouths during recess or lunch and another afternoon in Miss Webster's office. "I'll tell you after school when we get home."

It was a blissfully uneventful day and the girls enjoyed the novelty of once more riding on the bus and being the last four to get off just as that morning they had been the first four to get on. Charlie thought it conferred on them a certain distinction.

"We've never been first on and last off the bus before," said Charlie.

"Who cares?" said Natasha.

"It makes us special," said Charlie.

"You're living without a grown-up," said Marlin. "You're already special."

"Anyway, it does you no good to be special if no one knows why you're special," said Natasha.

"Yes, and let's keep it that way," said Fiona wryly.

They got a quick after-school snack in the kitchen and Fiona wrapped up the rest of the cake in foil.

"Now," she announced, "we are taking this next door."

"What—to that mean man in the trailer?" said Charlie in dismay.

"Yes. A plan has been forming at the back of my mind ever since Marlin joked that we should send letters to the aunts and uncles who wouldn't take us, offering to *pay* them to take us. It's been driving me crazy like an itch you can't reach but in the middle of the night it finally came to me. Last night I kept imagining situations where we would be found out because we had no grown-up pretending to be our guardian. And I thought of that man next door. He might not do it for free but I think he might if we offered to *pay* him."

"Why him?" asked Marlin.

"Well, he looks like he has no scruples and is in need of money. Also, he's close for emergencies. If we need someone to come over and pretend to be watching us."

Marlin nodded slowly. She could see the merit in this plan. "And the cake is to sweeten the deal? Good idea," she said, thinking of his stomach hanging over the belt of his pants. "He looks like he enjoys a good cake."

"I don't want to go. He's scary," said Charlie.

"You don't have to," said Fiona. "You can stay here and Natasha can too. Marlin too for that matter."

"Oh no," said Marlin. "I'm not letting you enter the lion's den alone. Come on." She hooked her arm through Fiona's and the two of them marched down the front steps carrying the foil-wrapped cake.

"You stay *in* the house, though, Charlie and Natasha!" yelled Marlin over her shoulder.

"And do your homework!" shouted Fiona.

When Fiona and Marlin got to the trailer and knocked on the door it took the man a long time to answer and when he did he looked fuzzy-headed.

"WHAT!" he roared just as he had a couple of days before. "Who are *you*?"

"We are Martha McCready's great-nieces," said Fiona patiently. "You met us before. Can we come in?"

"No," said the man, staggering back and landing on a couch opposite the open door. Fiona entered anyway, carefully stepping around the clutter of empty beer cans and bottles on the floor.

"Don't you throw away your garbage?" asked Marlin.

"Marlin," said Fiona warningly.

"What?" said the man, who seemed stunned. "Hey, who said you could come in?"

"We are paying you a friendly call. And speaking of paying," Fiona went on, "we have a proposition for you."

"Oh yeah?" said the man, dropping his head forward into his hands, his elbows resting on his knees. He looked mortally ill and smelled like wet wool.

"Yes. You see, we need a guardian," began Fiona. "We thought of you."

At this the man looked up and laughed uproariously. "You want me to be your *guardian*?"

"Yes," said Fiona. "In name only. We are living alone on Aunt Martha's property and we're going to be in trouble if people find out. We need a grown-up to sign things and generally assure everyone that we aren't alone. Even though we are."

"Well, you can forget about me. I hate children," said the man. "Horrible jam-handed sticky things. I didn't have any and I don't plan to. Go HOME."

"We brought you a cake," said Marlin, taking the foil package out of Fiona's hands, where she'd been tensely clutching it. "I made it myself. It's delicious."

"Oh…cake," said the man, sounding slightly mollified. He took it from Marlin's hands and put it in his lap. "Well, now, I don't remember the last time I had homemade cake. Can't say I object to *that*."

It took his shaking fingers a minute to open the foil and then he paused, stared down at it, and his face grew thunderous again as he said, "What's this? Is this a joke? This isn't cake. This is just mush!"

Fiona looked down. The almond cherry cake had not traveled well. The cherries had made a very wet cake to begin with and the trip over in her tense fingers had not improved matters. It was indeed a kind of pink mush in the foil.

"This is disgusting," he said. "I don't want this."

"*Disgusting?* Why *you*!" cried Marlin, leaning forward as if to charge him.

"Marlin, hush," said Fiona. "It must have gotten squashed coming over but it *tastes* fantastic. Taste it."

"No," said the man.

"Go on, taste it," encouraged Fiona.

"No, I changed my mind," said Marlin, taking it back from him. "He doesn't deserve my cake."

"You got that right," said the man.

"All right, listen, we started out wrong here," said

Fiona. "I think we need to exchange names properly. I'm Fiona, this is Marlin, my little sisters who stayed home are Natasha and Charlie. You met them the other day."

"Charlie's the one that cries," said the man with unexpected perspicacity.

"That's right!" said Fiona, as if awarding him a gold star.

"I remember her," said the man. "She was earth-shatteringly loud. God, I hate the sound of people crying. Particularly high-pitched little keeners like her."

"And your name is?" asked Fiona, hoping to move the conversation on from how much he hated children.

"Al," said the man.

"Al what? We can't just use Al as your name on forms and such."

"Al Farber, but you're not putting my name on anything because I won't do it."

"We don't need you to *do* anything. That's why it's such a sweet deal for you. We'll hardly bother you at all. We just need your name and phone number and if anyone calls you to check up on us, say you're the guardian. Or in the even more unlikely event someone comes to our house, you just run over for a very short time and pretend to be taking care of us. That's it."

"Forget it," said Al.

"We'll pay you," said Fiona.

"How much?"

"Twenty bucks a week."

"Twenty bucks a week?" Al started laughing. "I spend more than that on beer."

"Jeez, how much beer do you drink?" asked Marlin.

"None of your BUSINESS," barked Al. "You see, this is why I hate children. They've always got one nose in your business."

"Do you know children with more than one nose?" asked Marlin.

"What do you mean?"

"Well, you made it sound like one of their noses was in your business and one was somewhere else."

"Mother of God," said Al, dropping his head into his hands. "An editor!"

"Marlin, be quiet," said Fiona. "All Marlin meant by asking you about your, er, beer-drinking habits was that we can cover your beer costs. If they're not too exorbitant."

"Well!" said Al, looking up sharply at Fiona. "Someone with a vocabulary. I'd give you points for that if you weren't a child and I didn't hate children so much. But you are and I do so that's that."

Marlin looked around at the filthy trailer with its open cans of baked beans all sporting forks as if he opened one, stuck a fork in, ate a bit, discarded it, and then forgot about it and then opened a new one, stuck a fork in it, and left that one in a new place. The trailer was decorated in open cans with forks sticking out of them on all the shelves and flat surfaces. In a certain light, she decided, it might look like a modern art installation. Their father was always bringing them to modern art museums when they were stationed near big cities and explaining installations, which no matter how many she saw always seemed silly to her. This, she thought, was as good as any she'd seen. Then she shook herself and got back on point.

"And we'll bring you dinner every night," she added with sudden inspiration.

"Dinner?"

"A *hot* dinner," said Marlin.

"You can't cook," said the man, looking pointedly at the cake.

"THERE'S NOTHING WRONG WITH MY CAKE!" shouted Marlin.

"Nothing a garbage can couldn't solve," said Al.

"Besides, Fiona cooks dinner. She makes all kinds of tasty things, roast chicken and mashed potatoes, brisket with vegetables, vegetable soup, pork chops in mushroom sauce." Marlin rattled off things their mother used to make.

Al got a strange dreamy look in his eye.

"I haven't had a homemade pork chop in a long time," he said.

"Well, there you go. And all you have to do is pretend to be our guardian," said Fiona, leaping on this.

"All right," said Al. "We'll try it. But no mushy cakes."

"There's nothing WRONG..." began Marlin, decibels rising until Fiona hustled her out the door and down the steps.

"And you need to take us to town tomorrow to see our aunt's lawyer, Hiram Pennypacker," said Fiona, swiftly over her shoulder, hoping to end matters there.

"NO!" called Al from the top step of the trailer. "I won't take you to see that idiot."

"Please? You could just sit in the office and pose as our guardian and say nothing. I would do all the talking," said Fiona, stopping and turning to face him again. "St. Mary's By the Sea is a long walk. You could use my aunt's car. It's just sitting in the driveway."

"I've got my own truck, thank you very much. I don't need to borrow a car. But I won't go see that fool."

"Well, could you just drive us there and wait for us?"

"No."

"But I made an appointment," said Fiona. "And it's supposed to rain. We can't go in looking like drowned rats and we will if we have to walk an hour in the rain to get there."

"Your problem, not mine," said Al. "Now, does our deal include dinner tonight?"

"Only if you drive us tomorrow," said Marlin.

The girls stepped back in surprise as Al suddenly

pounded down the trailer steps, stomped across the yard, and went into a small shed. They were afraid they had pushed him too hard but in a minute, they saw what he had gone into the shed for as he wheeled a bike toward them.

"Here, you can buy this from me," he said. "Give you the bargain price of twenty bucks. It's a good bike. It's got a basket and everything."

"Wow," said Fiona, getting on it and pedaling around. It was a woman's bike, light blue with a white wicker basket, and seemed a little too froufrou to belong to Al. "This isn't yours, is it?"

"Do I look like someone who rides around on pretty bicycles?" he asked.

"Well, it looks in awfully good working order. Tires full of air, no rust on it. *Someone* has been using it."

"So?" said Al. "Are you saying if it were mine it wouldn't be in good working order?"

Fiona said nothing but eyed the refrigerator and tub sitting in the yard.

"You didn't steal it, did you?" she finally asked.

"STEAL IT!" roared Al. "You want it or not?"

"Yes please," said Fiona. "I'll bring you the twenty bucks and the beer money when we bring you dinner tomorrow. You don't get it tonight because you wouldn't drive us into town."

Al turned without a word and headed back to the trailer.

"Then we have a deal?" called Fiona.

"Yeah, yeah," he muttered.

"I need you to write down your name and address and phone number. No, forget the address, we'll fudge that for forms, it's probably better people think you now live with us."

"Oh, for Pete's sake," he said.

"You'll have to lie. I'm sorry about that," said Fiona. "But you will."

"Ha, I don't mind the lying," he said. "I mind the nuisance factor."

He found a pen and paper by the couch in the trailer and wrote his name and phone number down for Fiona and she and Marlin headed back home, Fiona wheeling the bike and Marlin still clutching the mushed almond cherry cake.

"And no more cakes!" he called out behind them. "Until you learn to make them properly!"

"I hate him," muttered Marlin as they walked up their driveway. When they got to the house she dropped the cake in the garbage can by the shed. "I don't want it after he had his dirty hands on it."

"Don't hate him, Marlin, he might be the saving of us," said Fiona. "But I wish you hadn't told him I could cook.

I can't make anything more complicated than grilled cheese or eggs."

"I know," said Marlin. "But that only occurred to me after I said you would."

"I guess now that we have the bike I may as well go see the lawyer alone," said Fiona. "Especially if it's supposed to rain. No sense all of us getting wet and only one of us can ride the bike."

"It's too bad we don't have bikes for everyone," said Marlin.

"Don't look a gift bike in the mouth," said Fiona. "It will be handy for errands. Especially with that basket. And twenty bucks seems cheap to me for a bike."

They stayed a bit in the driveway, taking turns riding it. Marlin appeared to be deep in thought as she rode in circles. Finally, she said, "You know, I think I could tweak that almond cherry cake recipe. It shouldn't have gotten all mushy like that. Less cherries maybe. Or drain them better."

"Don't let him get to you," advised Fiona.

"I'm not," said Marlin. "It's not about that…"

But she wouldn't say what it was about. She wasn't even sure herself, so they left it at that and went in to tell the others their good news.

Mr. Pennypacker

SATURDAY Fiona woke up full of buoyant spring fever and optimism. All the fruit trees were beginning to bloom. Poking up like candles on a birthday cake within the sea of green grass in the meadow were brown trunks topped by round pink puffs both dark and light. They were the kind of trees Charlie might draw, so perfectly round were the tops. The songbirds were calling each other from the meadow. It was the way, thought Fiona, that one might imagine heaven, a spring morning so soft yet lustrous, so bursting with life. Then she had the wish that if her parents were in heaven it was just like this. That perhaps they were all experiencing somehow on different planes the same morning together. The thought of this, her parents perhaps longing for them somewhere far away as they longed for their parents, made a tear run down her cheek but she brushed it off quickly. Anyhow, she decided, she couldn't really know anything for certain except what was before her and that was that the day was beautiful.

Natasha and Charlie were still asleep but Marlin and

Fiona sat on the front porch in sweaters in the soft March spring air, drinking hot cocoa from a mix that they'd found in Aunt Martha's cupboard.

"I've made an inventory of the freezer," said Marlin. "Either Aunt Martha thought children ate a great deal or she is one of those children of the depression that Mom used to talk about who have to squirrel away everything in case it happens again. There's a lot of meat. Lots of chicken. Bread. Frozen pizzas and potpies and that type of thing. There's frozen and fresh vegetables and cans of vegetables in the cabinets as well as canned baked beans and dry pasta, rice, et cetera. And she must have done some baking because she's got all the necessary baking supplies like baking powder and soda and even yeast, as you know. Really, all we need are milk and eggs and some butter because we're running low on those."

"Eggs we can get along the road," said Fiona. "I saw several egg stands from the bus. I can pick some up on the way home from town. I don't know what time I'll be back or how long it will take with Mr. Pennypacker to go through all of Aunt Martha's affairs. And then I still have to think of something to make for supper. I mean something that sounds like the stuff you promised Al."

"Never mind that," said Marlin. "I have been looking up recipes that use what we already have and I thought I would mess around with it."

"Really?" said Fiona. "You've never made dinner before."

"Well, neither have you," said Marlin. "Not anything complicated."

"True, true," said Fiona.

"I wish Mom had written down her recipes for us but I thought I could play around with making them from memory. The pork chops...there were mushrooms in it, I know, and there are pork chops in the freezer and mushrooms in the fridge..." Marlin drifted off in thought.

Reluctantly Fiona left the fragrant front porch and went inside to start a load of laundry. Then she sat down and made a detailed list of everything she could remember people doing to keep house. Laundry and vacuuming—Aunt Martha didn't have a vacuum but she had a broom. That would have to do. Washing the bathroom and kitchen. Really, it didn't seem too onerous. She figured if the four of them could blitz the house on Saturday they'd have Sunday free. Or blitz on Sunday and have Saturday free when it might be more fun to do things in town. Or at least one of them could go into town on the bike. Maybe they should take turns. Her head was swimming with ideas.

She went upstairs to find her one good outfit. She and her sisters had been around the world, each with the one large suitcase their parents allowed them. It had to contain everything they needed, toys, clothes, books. And they always had one outfit that was reserved for going to church or other occasions where their parents wanted them to be well-dressed. She decided she would wear hers: a nice pair of black pixie pants, a white silk shirt, and an elaborately embroidered green vest that her parents had bought her during their short sojourn in India. She put on running shoes and placed her good black flats in the bike basket to change into when she got to town. Then she was off for her ten o'clock appointment with Mr. Pennypacker.

Although they'd taken the bus down this road yesterday and walked it once, it was different on a bike. From her higher vantage point on the bike but slower speed than the bus she could see all kinds of things she'd missed, houses hidden in the woods, horses grazing in fields, orchards hidden behind a fringe of pine trees. It took half an hour on the bike to get as far as the school and another ten minutes to be at St. Mary's By the Sea's "downtown," which consisted of two intersecting streets. One street had a series of buildings with false fronts and it was here she found Mr. Pennypacker's office.

She parked her bike, changed her shoes, putting her running shoes in her backpack, and went inside. The receptionist took her name and pointed to a couch where she could sit and wait and in a few minutes Mr. Pennypacker came out. He was a short, delicate man who Fiona guessed to be about the same age Aunt Martha would have been. He had sharp features, bushy eyebrows, and a long white pointed beard. He wore a red vest and colorful pants, reminding her of something, but she couldn't think what.

"Ah!" He looked around. "Is no one with you?" he asked, ushering her into his inner office.

"No, just me," she said.

"Oh," he said. "I thought you'd have brought whatever grown-up traveled with you. We have a great deal of paperwork to go through. But your great-aunt made things easier by having everything ready before she died. She was a meticulous and responsible person and I am sorrier than I can say that she is gone. Now, I know she was planning to adopt the four of you but died, of course, before that happened. She didn't tell me what happened to your parents but I assumed they died together suddenly and that was why she was taking you in."

"Yes," said Fiona.

"As I say, your great-aunt had everything prepared for the eventuality of her death except a guardian appointed for the four of you in the case that anything happened to her. Biscuit?"

He held a plate with some rather chalky-looking Peek Freans cookies but Fiona took one politely and nibbled on the corner.

"Actually," she said, "she did take care of that. We do have a guardian."

"You don't say. It would have been nice if your guardian had come with you. It's highly irregular to be dealing with all the legalities with a fourteen-year-old. It would have been nice if Martha had told me about it too. I suppose she was going to but her unexpected death precluded that. Well, who is it?"

"His name is Al Farber," said Fiona.

She had expected a name to reassure Mr. Pennypacker but although up until that moment he had been smooth and lawyerly, he now stood up and roared, "WHAT? THAT DRUNKEN WASTREL!"

Fiona was so startled she couldn't say anything and her cookie fell from her hand into her lap.

"Did *he* tell you she'd appointed him or did that come from her?" asked Mr. Pennypacker, leaning forward and squinting his eyes suspiciously. "How did you hear that he was your guardian? I cannot see her choosing him! Not *him*. I could see him lying to you, though, if he was working some kind of an angle."

"No, no, we had to tell *him* he was the guardian in point of fact," said Fiona, thinking this part was at least close to the truth because now there was nothing for it but to elaborate with an outright lie. "We found her request to have him made the guardian in some papers in her underwear drawer when we were clearing out her stuff for the attic and we gave the papers to him."

She said this automatically because she kept things like chocolate bars or her diary or anything she didn't want to share with her sisters in her underwear drawer. But now the idea of finding things among her great-aunt's underwear made her blush and she wished she'd thought of another place to have found the papers.

"Well! She might have told *me*, her lawyer!" said Mr. Pennypacker, whose face had gone red and sweaty when he'd yelled. He sat back and wiped it with a handkerchief, trying to calm himself. "Well! I must say I don't know what she was thinking but then I seldom did. She was a wonderful woman but what you might call buttoned-up. Very private. No doubt it was his proximity that she felt made him suitable. Or perhaps he enlisted himself for the job."

Fiona snorted involuntarily at this.

"Well! All right. There are some things he will need to sign and I'll need to see paperwork showing he *is* who your aunt chose to be your legal guardian."

Fiona hadn't thought of this.

"All right," she said finally, wondering how she would get around this one.

"He's moving onto your property at some point, or has already, I assume?"

"Oh yes, he's looking into that," said Fiona vaguely.

The rest was just a lot of talk about the house and the money that had been left to them. It seemed a substantial amount although she had never dealt with large sums before. She had no idea what kind of bills there would be or how much it would cost the four of them to live. Her parents had always taken care of that. And after their death, the church and Mrs. Weatherspoon. Everything of Aunt Martha's had gone to Fiona and her sisters including, Mr. Pennypacker explained, the money from the sale of Aunt Martha's fishing boat if they could find a buyer. Mr. Pennypacker was handling the sale. Only some old fishing gear had gone to Al Farber.

"Why?" asked Fiona.

"Why?" he said. "I suppose because he used to trail your great-aunt around like a sick puppy while she fished, writing about her. She was a professional fisherman, as you know. He came here to do an article about her for the *New York Times*. That was a while ago when there weren't so many female professional fishermen going out alone. He ended up staying and writing a whole book about her. It was actually a bestseller for a time. Not that I ever thought it was much good. To capture your great-aunt on paper would not be an easy thing and I don't think in the end he really managed it, popular though the book might have been. She thought he would just pack up and go back to New York after he finished writing it and he should have but instead he bought the lot next door to her farm and parked that hideous trailer on it and stayed on and on.

There was some rumor he wanted to marry her. But she had more sense than to return his affections. He was more like...a...like a...STALKER!" Mr. Pennypacker spat out venomously.

"That's not what he told us," said Fiona. "That is, he didn't tell us they were, um, romantically involved."

"Well, I doubt they were, for her part anyhow," said Mr. Pennypacker smugly.

"He said they never spoke to each other."

"Well, there you have it. You see," said Mr. Pennypacker, "shameless liar."

Fiona began to wonder if St. Mary's By the Sea attracted liars. Miss Webster, Al Farber, and now the four of them.

"What was the book called?" asked Fiona.

"Oh, I forget. She probably has a copy in her library. He certainly has a copy or two. Wastrel," he said again, staring off over Fiona's right shoulder looking grim. "Anyhow, that's no doubt why she left him the fishing gear. He was on her boat for days at a time writing and she taught him to fish, I believe. Started out Mr. Fancy Pants Big-City Boy from New York, looking down his nose at all of us yokels and ends up wanting to fish like her—with her. I guess she scotched those plans. That woman always did exactly what she liked. And alone. For the most part. Well! That's all for now. Bring me that paperwork. Here, I'll walk you out."

They went outside, where it was clouding up.

"How did you get here?" asked Mr. Pennypacker, looking at the sky.

"Biked," said Fiona, pointing to the bicycle.

"Ah, Martha's bike," said Mr. Pennypacker.

"*Martha's* bike?" said Fiona. "This belonged to *my aunt*?"

"Yes, of course, what did you think?" asked Mr. Pennypacker, looking surprised by the question. "Everything you find on that property was hers. She almost never took her car into town unless she had heavy things to haul back. She loved that old bike. Kept it in fighting trim too. You'd better hurry. Looks like rain to me."

Fiona thanked him and headed to the grocery store for milk and butter, spluttering to herself, *"Martha's bike! Martha's!"*

Then she headed home, stopping to get eggs at an egg stand.

When she got back she found Marlin in the kitchen busily putting together another cake, flour splattered about and recipes she'd copied from the internet spread everywhere. Natasha and Charlie were sitting at the counter watching her.

Fiona told them everything.

"He wrote for the *New York Times*?" said Marlin. "Wow. Who would have thought?"

"Yes, and Mr. Pennypacker called him a waste troll," said Fiona.

Charlie and Natasha laughed. "Waste troll, waste troll," chanted Charlie.

"Don't say that to his face," warned Fiona. "We need him, remember."

Natasha leapt up and went to the bookcases in the living room, where she searched the shelves, climbing on the little library ladder going up and down until she shouted, "FOUND IT!" She triumphantly pulled out a volume with Al Farber's name on the spine. "It's called *Martha's Boat*." She handed the book to Fiona to look at and while Marlin cooked, Fiona began to read it aloud to them.

At the end of the first chapter Marlin, who was mixing a coating for the pork chops she was baking, said, "Wow, what happened to him after he wrote this? He was a good writer. You'd never expect him to end up in a trailer with baked bean cans everywhere. The person who wrote this doesn't sound like Al. Maybe it's a different Al Farber."

"No," said Fiona thoughtfully. "It's the same. Mr. Pennypacker said." She opened the fridge to look for something for a snack. She had missed lunch and all the biking had made her ravenous. There was a large bowl of some kind of slaw and she stuck a fork in to taste it. "Did *you* make this?" she asked Marlin in amazement.

"Yep," said Marlin, beaming happily. "I found this recipe for slaw but I thought it was too bitter and I just started adding things I thought would work."

"This is fantastic," said Fiona.

"I like to cook," said Marlin. "I just never knew it before. Someone was always cooking for us. And I'm also tweaking this pork chop recipe that I found that started out sounding the way Mom used to make them. But I think...I can improve on it," she murmured, reading the recipe and throwing a shake of this spice and a shake of that into the coating mix.

"Well, if your pork chops are as good as your slaw, at least Al won't be able to complain about the dinners we bring," said Fiona.

The girls spent the rest of the day in happy activities. Natasha had found a *Wildlife of British Columbia* book and was engrossed in the bird section while lying on the hammock on the back porch, lazily looking up each new bird as it flew by the porch.

Charlie was climbing all the fruit trees one by one as if introducing herself to them. They still didn't know what kind they were. Natasha thought they should look them up in Aunt Martha's *Trees of British Columbia* book but Charlie said it would be more exciting to wait and see what kind of fruit magically materialized in the summer.

Marlin was contentedly engrossed in cooking and baking and Fiona sat down at Martha's computer and went through her records trying to figure out what bills lay ahead and how the online banking worked.

At suppertime Marlin put pork chops, oven fries, and slaw into a large food container.

"Aren't you giving him a piece of that cake?" asked Charlie, pointing to the cake Marlin had spent all morning fussing over.

"No, he doesn't deserve my cake. He's never getting cake from me again," said Marlin.

Fiona sighed. When Marlin held a grudge, it could be a long time before the person in question was forgiven. She took the food container from her and biked it down the driveway and next door.

Al answered the door the way he always did, by throwing it open and shouting "WHAT!" But Fiona had decided to do the intimidating herself for a change.

First, she handed him twenty dollars.

"What's this?" he asked.

"You remember the deal," she said.

"I remember the deal being for beer money. I haven't given you my beer bill yet."

"It's not something we can leave open-ended. You might decide to drink us into the poorhouse. Twenty bucks," said Fiona. "Take it or leave it."

"Hmm," grumbled Al. "And where's the money for the bike?"

"You're not getting any money for the bike," said Fiona. "I saw Mr. Pennypacker today and he told me that bike was my aunt's. My aunt left everything but the fishing gear to us so that bike is ours as you well know. I'm still not convinced how you ended up with it, if you stole it or—"

"*STOLE* it!" roared Al. "I never stole anything in my life. Listen, you kids have got to stop thinking I go around stealing bikes. Mother of God! I worked on it as a favor for her. It had burst a tire. That twenty dollars was just to cover my costs."

"How do I know that's true?" asked Fiona.

"You don't," said Al. "But how do I know this little arrangement you've dreamt up isn't going to land me in big trouble? I don't. I guess we're just going to have to trust each other. To a certain degree. But hey, if you can't trust me, no skin off my nose. We can end the deal right here. I didn't ask for any of this." He started to close the door but before he could, Fiona swiftly opened the food container to display Marlin's delicious-looking food. The aroma of pork chops in thick mushroom gravy and potatoes and coleslaw drifted up. Even she wanted to stick a finger in and start tasting things.

"Twenty dollars a week and dinner and you absorb the cost for the bike repair since it still feels to me like you tried to sell me a bike that was already mine," said Fiona.

Al thought for a minute but the pork chops won out. He took the food container without another word.

Fiona turned on her heel and left before he changed his mind.

She biked home to her own dinner.

When they'd all settled at the kitchen table, Fiona lifted a water glass up and said, "To our first week. So far so good."

"So far so good," the others repeated, and then the girls dove into Marlin's delicious food.

"The thing I'm most proud of," Marlin said, "is that nothing you're eating comes from Mom's recipes. Or Mrs. Weatherspoon's! Or even the internet. I'm tweaking everything. I'm developing my own cooking style. And I think I fixed the almond cherry cake recipe so it doesn't end up so goopy! This one has pineapple as well as cherries but I drained the cherries and tossed them in flour before adding them and I added a pineapple-coconut mélange to the bottom of the pan."

"Ooooo, mélange," teased Natasha. "You even use cooking words."

"I'm not sure that's a cooking term," said Marlin seriously. "I think I may have made that one up but it should be a cooking term if it isn't."

"It's an awfully good cake," said Fiona, taking a second piece. "It rivals any of Mrs. Weatherspoon's."

"Yes, see, the texture is grainier and lighter than the last cake I made and the fruit is more evenly distributed," said Marlin wonderingly as she picked her piece apart with her fork to study it.

"I don't care about any of that," said Charlie. "Just so long as it tastes good."

Then Fiona told them everything she had learned at Mr. Pennypacker's. "I think we're going to be okay," she finished cautiously. "Aunt Martha's boat is up for sale so we'll get some more money from that as well."

She didn't tell them what was worrying her, which was that the money they had, while seeming to be enough, mightn't be. Not in the long run. She had not counted on so many bills and she knew she'd have to buy everyone clothes and shoes again in the fall. She also suspected there would be many more unanticipated expenses as time went by. Every time she had a budget made up she remembered something else. But for now, she said to herself, they were okay. Don't borrow trouble, her mother had always said. She sighed. Well, she'd try not to.

Billy Bear

ALL went quietly and well that first month. Spring carpeted the meadows in blue wildflowers. Migrating Canada geese coming home passed over the house squawking each morning.

"Just think," Natasha said in wonder, "we're seeing Canada geese in *Canada*!"

Fiona told Miss Webster about Al's role as the fake guardian one Sunday when she was making her inspection. She didn't expect Miss Webster to be thrilled with this news and she wasn't.

"The more people who are privy to this deceit, the more dangerous," she said.

"I know," said Fiona. "But we couldn't help it."

"Well, let him be the last," said Miss Webster.

"We'll try," said Fiona.

Miss Webster nodded, saying she was otherwise impressed with how well the girls were doing on their own, and left small gifts of school supplies and school hoodies for all of them.

"She's awfully nice," said Marlin after she'd gone. "I wonder why she never married."

"She could still marry," said Fiona.

"She's kind of old," said Charlie.

"At least thirty," agreed Marlin.

"Maybe she's like Aunt Martha," said Natasha. It fascinated them, this great-aunt they had never known but the accoutrements of whose life they seemed to have settled into. Almost as if they had settled into her *life* like being dragged along in the wake of her boat.

"Well, Aunt Martha could have married," said Fiona. "Mr. Pennypacker and Al Farber both seem to have wanted her. I think Mr. Pennypacker carried a torch for Aunt Martha and was jealous of Al. That was my impression. And she didn't seem to have cared for either of them."

"Maybe that's what made Al so cranky," suggested Charlie.

"For years?" said Marlin skeptically. "Because that book was published ten years ago. Maybe he was so cranky to begin with she didn't want anything to do with him."

"It would be interesting to know the whole story," agreed Fiona. "He doesn't talk about any of that in the book. He just talks about her fishing."

"*I'm* not asking him," said Marlin.

"He does write that Martha said she was married to her boat," said Natasha. "Maybe that's a clue. And maybe

Miss Webster is married to her job the way Martha was married to her boat and that's why she isn't married."

"According to the book, Martha loved being alone and she loved being alone at sea," said Fiona. "I don't think Miss Webster is like that. She strikes me as more of a people person."

"I like her best of everyone we've met here," said Charlie. "If I could pick someone to be our guardian for real it would be her. She slipped me and Natasha chocolate bars when she saw us at lunch the other day."

"Well, we don't get to pick a guardian from just anyone we want," said Fiona practically. "We're lucky to get anyone to even pretend to be one. Even if it is a waste troll like Al."

"He's like one of the wild beasts," said Charlie.

"He certainly is," said Marlin. "The way he hollers every time I knock on the door to give him his dinner."

Marlin and Fiona took turns delivering Al's dinners and despite the fact that he must have known by then that it was them at six o'clock each night at his door, his method of answering never varied.

"Wild beast, wild beast, wild beast troll," chanted Charlie.

"There are no wild beasts for us to be afraid of," said Fiona as she did every time Charlie brought them up. "They're all far back in the woods."

Fiona worried about Charlie and what seemed her increasing nervous nattering about wild beasts. Charlie still never went out the front door without peering into tree branches for crouching cougars. She even scanned the waters for shark fins when they went to the beach even though all of them had assured her that the local waters didn't contain sharks. Fiona wondered if everything Charlie had been through in the last year had made her yet more fearful and if there was something she should be doing about it. Maybe Charlie needed some kind of professional help which they couldn't anyway afford. How could you tell when someone had tipped over the edge from normally fearful to pathologically fearful? Fiona was therefore thrilled when as April sped by, Charlie, after Fiona had taught her how to adjust the seat for her shorter legs, began of her own volition to take the bike up and down the driveway and down the road and back. At first, she wanted Fiona or Marlin to walk alongside her and keep a watch on the surrounding forest for wolves and bears that might be stalking her but now she seemed content to go alone. She was confident enough that one Thursday after school Fiona gave her the job of dragging the wheeled garbage can to the end of their driveway as she had noticed most people on the street did for pickup early the next morning rather than dragging it down at six a.m. when the garbagemen began their route on

Farhill Road. Whenever possible Fiona tried to apportion the many chores fairly but there weren't a lot of chores she felt Charlie could handle yet and she was happy to give her this one.

"You sure you can do this?" asked Fiona. "It's got wheels but you have to drag it a long way."

"Yep," said Charlie proudly. "And after, I'm taking the bike out."

"Good for you, Charlie," said Fiona. She went inside pleased that everyone, even Charlie, seemed to be adjusting to their new life.

Fiona heard the garbage can being dragged and then Charlie pedaling off down the driveway and breathed a sigh of relief.

Charlie biked down the drive and along the road where many other people's garbage cans were already out. She didn't tell Fiona but she still kept one eye out for things in the woods but the more she biked without seeing anything fearful, the less she worried about it. So she was happily tooling along when at first she thought she saw an oddly shaped black garbage can a few drives down. Then the black can moved. Charlie held her breath and stopped abruptly, one foot on a pedal and one on the road. After looking for one for so long, she could not believe the thing of nightmares stood before her. Right there in the open.

She looked searchingly at it as if expecting it to turn back into an oddly shaped garbage can but the bear stared back at her instead. Someone who knew bears could have told her it was not a very big black bear but it didn't feel small to Charlie. She screamed and leapt off her bike, running to the nearest shelter, which was Al's trailer. She didn't even bother knocking but charged inside, where Al was lying on the couch listening to a podcast.

"What the *HECK*!" he roared.

"THERE'S A BEAR!" roared Charlie even louder.

"Where?" asked Al, sitting up calmly and removing his earbuds.

"Outside," she said. "He has taken the top off someone's garbage can."

"Sounds about right," said Al.

They looked out the window to where they could see a bear ambling along dragging a bag of garbage.

"Oh, that's just Billy Bear," Al said, and lay down again.

Charlie stood glued to the window trembling. When she didn't leave Al sat up again. "I said you don't have to worry. Billy Bear has been around since he was a cub. He knows when people put their garbage out. Watch. I'll show you what to do when you meet a bear."

Al went outside, planted his feet solidly in his driveway, and said in normal tones, "Okay, Billy, you've finished your Oreos, now it's time to go."

The bear looked up at Al. He was sitting peacefully taking apart his bag of garbage and he seemed disappointed and even a bit sad to have this activity interrupted but he stood up resignedly and slowly ambled off into the woods again.

"There, see," said Al, coming back inside. "Bears are way more afraid of you than you are of them. Poor Billy had his supper interrupted. Oh well, at least he got to finish his Oreos."

Al lay down again but when Charlie didn't leave, he sat up and said, "Now listen," but at that moment his phone rang.

"Who the *HECK*," said Al, going to his shelf where the phone lay and picking it up. "WHAT!" he roared, his phone-answering style apparently the same as his door-answering. "What? What?" he kept repeating. "Well, she *did*. No, you're the one she wouldn't leave in charge of a bunch of kids. That's right. She didn't accept your proposal either so I guess that makes us equal. Well, maybe she didn't want to marry a garden gnome. What is that in *reference* to? Have you looked in the mirror lately? Oh yeah, well, guess what, I don't have to prove it. I don't have to prove anything. And where I live is my own business." And he hung up.

Al sat muttering to himself and then, when he saw Charlie still standing there staring at him, her eyes huge, he said, "What have the lot of you gotten me into? Now that garden gnome of a lawyer wants to see proof I'm your guardian. He's threatening to come over if I don't go to see him. I've told him over the phone numerous times that I am, but oh no, he won't take *my* word for it! And he keeps asking when I'm moving onto your property. Well, what a tangled web we weave!"

When Charlie still didn't say anything, Al said, "What's the matter, bear got your tongue?"

Before she thought Charlie blurted out, "Does he call you a waste troll because the bear eats your garbage?"

"A what? A waste troll? Who calls me a waste troll?"

"Mr. Pennypacker. That's what Fiona said."

"A *waste troll*?" said Al, clearly flummoxed. "When did he call me a waste troll? What the heck!"

"You called him a garden gnome," Charlie pointed out. "My mother said you should never call people names."

"Out. Go home! I've had all I can take for one day. I'm not running a day care center."

But Charlie, instead of leaving, just sat down in the tiny booth with the kitchen table. "No," she said quietly. "I'm scared."

"I told you that bear doesn't want anything to do with you."

"He's still out there," said Charlie.

"Unlikely," said Al.

"No," repeated Charlie.

"Oh, for God's sake," said Al. "Come on. I'll walk you home."

Charlie followed Al reluctantly out the door and down the broken trailer steps. She hung on to the hem of his T-shirt, which he chose to ignore, and together they walked to the street. Al stopped to pick up the mess the bear had left behind: cartons and Kleenex and cans strewn along the side of the road. He shoved it into his garbage can while Charlie picked up her abandoned bike and then they continued up the road to the children's long driveway, with Charlie wheeling the bike because she was afraid to mount it and ride. Natasha had told her never to run from wild animals because they would think you were prey and chase you. Charlie had forgotten that the second she saw the bear but now she remembered and vowed not to make that mistake again. She was lucky she hadn't excited what Natasha had called the prey drive of the wild beast. She wasn't going to press her luck by riding her bike. The bear was most likely stalking her and Al, waiting his chance. Just hoping they would run or bike swiftly so he could chase them.

When they got to the front steps of the house Marlin said, "Oh hey, I was about to call you in, Charlie. Good timing. I'm putting dinner on the table. You might as well eat here with us, Al, instead of having us pack up your supper."

"Don't want to," said Al with his usual charm.

"We saw a BEAR!" said Charlie.

"Really!" said Marlin, her eyes growing huge.

"Oh, for God's sake," said Al. "It was only *Billy* Bear. He lives here. I've known him since he was a cub. Let me tell you something, that bear scares me less than the lot of you. Just give me my supper and I'll get out of here. Poor Billy."

So Marlin packed up a food container with meatloaf and mashed potatoes and green bean casserole and Al grunted and headed for home.

Charlie told them all about the bear at dinner and Natasha said she had done the right thing going to the nearest house.

"They're not Disney bears," she said. "No matter what Al says. A bear might not attack you but it might. That's the thing about bears."

"Don't scare her," warned Fiona. "She'll never go outside again."

"Better to be safe than sorry," said Natasha.

Then Charlie told them about Al calling Mr. Penny-packer a garden gnome and Fiona, who'd been taking a gulp of her milk, laughed until it came out her nose.

"What's so funny?" asked Marlin.

"Wait until you see him," said Fiona. "He actually does look exactly like a garden gnome. He's short and he has the same kind of face and white beard. When I saw him, he was even wearing a red vest and I was trying to think what he reminded me of."

"Al got mad that Mr. Pennypacker called him a waste troll," said Charlie, who having calmed down was now reveling in being the one who'd had the adventure and a story to relate. She was seldom the one in the family with interesting gossip.

"Oh, Charlie, I told you not to tell him that," said Fiona.

"I couldn't help it," said Charlie. "The bear scared all thoughts out of my head."

Fiona just sighed and hoped it wouldn't come back to haunt them later and then they all finished dinner, did their homework, and went to bed.

But Charlie got up every ten minutes for the first hour, looking out the window for bears in the moonlight. She didn't really expect to see one but the third time she got up there was Billy Bear, knocking over the extra garbage can they kept by the back shed. When he found it empty he first rolled it for a way as if it were a toy and when he'd gotten all the fun out of that that he could, he went across the meadow and for a moment it looked to Charlie like he was dancing. He stood on his hind legs and his front legs swayed back and forth as if to music only he could hear. It was such an unexpected thing to see. Such a wondrous thing that it took Charlie's breath away. She didn't even think to call the others but realized for the first time that things happened when she was sleeping, wondrous things, almost all of which she would never see or know. She was privileged just this once to witness something she would not have suspected took place while all the world but her remained unaware. *I wonder if he dances on the day the garbage goes out because it's his favorite day,* thought Charlie sleepily, *or if it's the moonlight making him dance.* Maybe when the moon was full it scattered energy in the form of moonbeams that made all the forest and ocean creatures dance. She had a vision of squirrels and otters and seals, starfish, sea anemones and whales and cougars and wolves, all dropping whatever they were doing to perform an intricate interconnected sequence of steps brought on by moonbeam madness. Or maybe they weren't controlled by the moon, maybe they chose to dance because they loved the light on such nights. Or maybe it wasn't all creatures. Maybe it was Billy Bear alone. Not just any bear, any more than she was just any child. But a unique bear. Maybe all bears were unique to themselves. It suddenly occurred to her that bears were creatures of thought too and Billy might well like moonlight. He might like all kinds of things. That a bear's head might be filled with things besides ways to frighten and kill her, was a new thought. That his mind might be full of all kinds of things just as hers was. The things he loved, the things he feared, the things he missed, the new things he was puzzling out. That any creature's life was made up of the wonderful jumble of what they held in their head and their heart. That the things Billy loved were stored away and treasured: garbage, moonlight, other bears in his family, honey, the smell of spring, the warm den when winter came, the feel in summer of a wet cool creek running past his furry legs, that first blissful moment after a long day when sleep snuck in and claimed him. That he was a creature enjoying the life he had somehow miraculously been given, the same as she.

But our tastes will always be different when it comes to garbage was her last sleepy thought.

And then it was another morning and all the different things that meant for Charlie. And all the different things that meant for the bear.

Donald Pettinger

ONE of the first rules Fiona made for all of them when they started school was that they could make friends but they could not bring them home.

"Too chancy," she said. "Someone coming upstairs is bound to see the four of us set up in the only two bedrooms and wonder why there is no evidence of a guardian. And people talk. It's bad enough we now have two grown-ups who know and Mr. Pennypacker, who is nagging Al about seeing legal proof of guardianship, which we haven't got. I'm hoping he forgets about it but if he doesn't, I don't know what we're going to do. Frankly, I'm surprised we've made it into April without anyone else finding out. I think we are going to have to lay low and as much as possible be invisible."

Everyone had agreed that this was prudent and that they would meet friends on neutral territory or go to the friends' homes.

Fiona thought the plan was working well until one day Charlie burst into tears the minute they were off the school bus and headed down their driveway.

Now what? thought Fiona wearily.

"Ashley won't play with me anymore and it's all your fault," yelled Charlie as she slammed into the house.

"What do you mean my fault?" asked Fiona, following her inside.

"She keeps asking to play at my house. We always play at her house. And I keep saying no so now she won't play with me at all!"

Charlie had taken to going to Ashley's house on Saturdays. Fiona would take her there on the handlebars of the bike on her way to do the grocery shopping in town and then pick her up with the bike later in the day.

Ashley's mother said the same thing to Fiona each time she showed up: "Have your mother stop by to say hello next time she's around," and Fiona would have to remind her that they didn't have a mother, they had a guardian. And Ashley's mother would then say, "Oh yes, dear, well, have him stop by to say hello."

Fiona always smiled inwardly at the idea of Ashley's mother saying hello and Al barking "WHAT!" Once she had actually snorted out loud at the thought and had to cover it with a cough. But the important thing was that Ashley's mother never pursued it beyond that.

Now Charlie was sobbing angrily and stomping around her bedroom so Fiona went back outside and sat down on the front-porch steps, dropping her head into her hands.

Suppose all the girls in Charlie's class felt the same way Ashley did and Charlie never got invited to the sleepovers or birthday parties? Fiona was beyond such things. All Marlin seemed to care about anymore was inventing recipes, writing them down and then tweaking them, and taking photos of her meals. Fiona was the tiniest bit worried that this was becoming obsessive but worrying about *that* seemed a luxury compared to her other worries. And Natasha cared less about people than the natural world, birds in particular. But she had always been that way. She made friends easily at school and fit in and didn't care if they couldn't come to the house. She was just as happy to be alone. It was Charlie's social life that was the issue. Charlie had always had a close friend, a best friend, wherever she lived. Otherwise she just sat in her room after school and moped. Fiona knew her mother was relieved when Charlie had picked someone upon whom to confer this honor in whatever new place they were living. Once Charlie had this best friend she seemed to relax. Fiona would have liked to tell Charlie to simply pick another friend but she knew it didn't work this way for Charlie. Charlie spent a long time sussing out the situation and was very particular about who she chose.

Fiona thought and thought of a way to solve the problem but the only solution she could come up with was that Ashley could come home on the bus with them. Then they could drive her home afterward rather than have her mother get her and possibly twig to the fact that no adult was on-site. It was either that or making Al come over when Ashley's mother swung by and pretend to be a calm courteous upright citizen who lived with them and she didn't think she had a tinker's chance of that. But perhaps she could arrange for the former. She stood up reluctantly. She didn't see a way to avoid it. She headed down the driveway to ask for help.

Fiona braced herself and knocked on Al's door.

"WHAT!" he roared before he even got to the door.

"Don't you ever go outside?" she asked him as the door swung open and he appeared squinting in the sunlight.

"Why would I?" he barked.

She thrust an arm out, palm upward, and gestured in an arc as if to display the lilacs in bloom, the creeping rosy flowers that blanketed all the rocky outcroppings, the forsythia, the fruit trees, the birds calling, and even the gentle buzzing of the bees.

"Is that why you came over? To goad me into some sort of outside recreational program?" he said.

"No, of course not. I've got a problem with Charlie only you can solve." She hoped if she put it to him thus he would be flattered into agreeing.

He nodded to her as if to say, go on.

"She wants to invite a friend, Ashley, over and I don't want Ashley's mother picking her up and figuring out that we are living without benefit of a grown-up, for obvious reasons. So the easiest way to solve that is for us to drive Ashley home so her mother doesn't come at all."

"And by us you mean me?"

"Yes."

"No. Don't provide taxi service. Not in the contract," said Al, and prepared to slam the door but Fiona stuck her foot in it.

"Naturally I don't expect you to do this for free," she said. "I can pay you or you can tell me what you would like in return."

"Cookies," said Al without thinking.

"Really? You'll do it for *cookies*?" Fiona asked in surprise. She had expected to have to spend a great deal more time wheedling him with imaginative offers. Cookies were easy.

"That's what I said."

"Okay. What kind?"

"Chocolate chip. And they have to be freshly baked."

"All right."

"And I want Marlin to make them, not you."

"Yes, of course."

"Don't of course me. Don't think I haven't figured out what goes on over there. If Marlin can't make dinner for some reason, you make it, don't you? You don't think I know when that happens? Burnt mac 'n' cheese? Pot roast with the consistency of shoe leather? Those are the meals you cook. Or rather you try and fail to cook. When it comes to cooking, you suck."

Fiona looked at him. What he said was absolutely true. She had had to take over for Marlin on occasion and she did suck at cooking but she was amazed that Al was clear-headed enough to have figured this out. Most of the time he looked as if he couldn't think his way out of a paper bag. On the other hand, she had to remember that he did once write for the *New York Times*.

"All right," she said. "So, can I tell Charlie she can have Ashley over on Thursday? Will you be free to take her home? Say around five-thirty? As if you'd just gotten home from work?"

"Do I look like I have a busy social calendar?" snapped Al, and slammed the door.

When Fiona got home she told Marlin about her conversation with Al.

"Really?" said Marlin in pleased tones as she put popovers in the oven and took out the last of the small roasts they had found in the freezer. "He can tell the difference between your meals and mine?"

"Marlin, a pig could tell the difference between your dinners and mine. And he wants cookies. He didn't say how many but I say give him two dozen to be on the safe side. I don't want any last-minute backing out on his part."

"Sure. Cookies are easy. What kind?"

"Chocolate chip."

"So boring," said Marlin resignedly.

"These aren't for experimentation, these cookies. These are a bribe so stick to the recipe."

"Whatever," said Marlin. "He'd be better off if I didn't stick to the recipe. The ones I've been making for our lunches have been fantastic because I change things up. You know, I'm extremely talented at cooking, and very good at baking, but I think I have a kind of genius when it comes to cookies. Those dried cranberries and orange-peel bits made all the difference to the almond cookies."

"They were great but make basic ones for Al. We don't want him reneging on a macadamia nut technicality."

"Philistine," said Marlin, and returned to copying notes into the file she kept in Aunt Martha's MacBook Air, which was now always open on the kitchen counter when she was playing with recipes so she could keep track of what she was adding or changing with exact measurements.

Then Fiona went to tell Charlie, who immediately called Ashley with the good news.

———

When Natasha, Marlin, and Fiona got to the school bus on Thursday they found a small blond girl standing next to Charlie. Charlie and the girl were yammering away at each other and hardly noticed them. The four sisters usually sat together at the back of the bus. But Charlie steered

Ashley to seats away from her sisters. When Charlie didn't need to cling to her sisters, Fiona always breathed a sigh of relief.

As soon as they got home, Ashley and Charlie ran into the meadow to play. Fiona took the garbage can to the street for Charlie and was busy with homework and paying bills and so it wasn't until an hour had passed that she thought to check on them. It was then that her heart went immediately into her throat. Sitting in the middle of the fenced meadow looking perfectly happy was Billy Bear, sorting through a bag of garbage he had dragged there.

"MARLIN!" called Fiona so sharply that Marlin came at a run from where she was baking the chocolate chip cookies.

Fiona pointed at the bear.

Marlin gasped. "Where are the girls? Where are Charlie and Ashley?"

Fiona pointed again. "In that tree. The one not ten feet from where the bear has settled."

"Oh no!" said Marlin. "Do you think they know the bear is there?"

"How could they not?" said Fiona. "They must be terrified. They must be keeping still hoping the bear doesn't notice them. I've got to go out and scare it away."

"Here," said Marlin, running back to the kitchen and grabbing pots and spoons. "We'll bang on these."

They ran to the back-porch steps and started banging

away. The bear looked thunderstruck for a second and in a panic left his pile of garbage and began to run around and around the meadow but the wind must have blown the gate to the meadow shut. The bear had no way out.

"We have to open the gate," said Fiona.

"You can't, the bear is too close," said Marlin, for the bear had decided there was no immediate threat, gone back for his garbage, and settled himself right next to the gate.

They stared at him for another moment silently.

"What are we going to do?" whispered Marlin, terrified.

"Call Miss Webster," said Fiona decisively.

She ran for the phone and dialed Miss Webster's number. When Miss Webster heard Fiona's voice squeaking, "Miss Webster?" she barked, "What's wrong?"

Fiona told her about the bear and Miss Webster, who didn't seem to feel like Al that bears were more afraid of you than you were of them, said, "I'm calling the conservation officer. Keep an eye on things and if Ashley and Charlie try to get out of the tree, yell to them to stay in it."

"Yes, we've done that," said Fiona.

Natasha, who had joined them at this point and was listening, said, "Bears can climb trees."

"Bears can climb trees," relayed Fiona.

"Well, he's got garbage," said Miss Webster. "If the girls don't threaten him, he has no reason to go after them. Now hang up. I'll be over as soon as I've made the call."

Fiona ran outside again to tell the girls Miss Webster was calling the conservation officer and then coming over.

Miss Webster arrived minutes later and very shortly after, a tall handsome man in his thirties wearing a khaki uniform showed up. He had a flatbed truck with a crane and a bear cage on it and he carried a rifle.

Miss Webster and the girls stood on the back porch biting their knuckles while the conservation officer introduced himself as Donald Pettinger before walking in a relaxed way to the meadow as if it were a squirrel he was going after.

"Isn't he afraid?" breathed Natasha.

"He does this all the time," said Miss Webster, putting her hands on Natasha's shoulders.

"Girls," he called from the fence to Ashley and Charlie. "We've got a bit of a bear situation here."

The girls said nothing. Charlie, in the tree, was afraid if she spoke Billy Bear would see her. She figured they were safe as long as they were not spotted.

As soon as the bear saw Donald Pettinger, he panicked again and leapt up, running in a strange lope around the big meadow. Mr. Pettinger opened the gate.

"Is he going to chase him out?" asked Fiona.

"No, that bear knows where to find food now. He can't let him go," said Miss Webster.

Mr. Pettinger closed the gate behind himself, walked into

the fenced meadow, put his rifle up, and fired but missed. This terrified the bear, who began slamming himself into the fence, but it was a high solid deer fence and the bear simply bounced off and in his frenzy, ran again in circles.

Charlie, watching him, began to lose her fear in pity for the plight of the trapped and panicked bear. Now instead of fearing for herself she feared for him. The more frantically he ran, the more she pitied him.

"Oh, don't shoot him!" she cried at last. "Please don't shoot him."

But the conservation officer ignored her, lifted his rifle, and this time he aimed true and the bear fell silent in the blue wildflowers.

Charlie began to cry. But now she was crying for the bear. For all the springs he would not see again, all the moonlight shining without him, no more garbage days, no more feeling the tickle of running creeks on his furry legs, no more summer sunsets or wet dawn grasses on his paws. Tears flowed from her eyes in a way they never had before. She didn't know who she was crying for; it seemed to be for Billy Bear but for herself and for everyone else too.

Ashley looked at her uncomprehendingly. "He got it," she said. "We can get down now." And she shinnied down the tree but Charlie stayed there until the conservation officer walked over.

"Need a hand?" he asked.

"I didn't want you to do that," sobbed Charlie. "I didn't want you to kill him."

"I didn't," said Mr. Pettinger in surprise. "I sedated him. That was a tranquilizer dart. He'll wake up just fine when it wears off. I'm going to drive my truck into the meadow, hook him up to that crane you see there. I'll haul him into the cage and take him an hour away to a lonelier stretch of forest where he can live."

"But he won't be at home," said Charlie sadly. "He won't know where he is."

"No," said the man, "he won't. But at least he will be able to live somewhere. Sometimes a fed bear is a dead bear. Because they hurt someone before we can relocate them. At least he was spared that."

By this point the others had all come walking cautiously across the field toward the downed bear as if they were worried he might come awake at any moment, leap up, and start his frantic scurrying around again.

"Can't you just leave him here?" asked Charlie. "I mean in the forest down the road?"

"Why, Charlie," said Miss Webster. "I think you like that bear."

"He lived his whole life here. Al said he knew him from when he was a cub. He probably has his whole family in the woods here somewhere," said Charlie. "His mother and father and sisters and brothers won't know what has happened to him."

Fiona had a feeling Charlie was going to forget herself and start talking about sisters scattered to the four winds because no one came forward to care for them and give away their situation to Mr. Pettinger so she interrupted and said to him, "Would you like a cookie? Marlin made them and they just came out of the oven."

"I'd better get the bear in the truck," said Mr. Pettinger.

"I want to go home," whispered Ashley to Charlie. "Why did Miss Webster come?"

"Oh, I'm an old family friend," said Miss Webster, overhearing. She and Fiona shot each other a sudden look. "Always happy to help out. Now, Mr. Pettinger, can you tell these girls where the bear is going?"

"Would you like to see where I'm taking the bear?" asked Mr. Pettinger. "Or you? You're the grade school principal, aren't you?"

"How did you know?" asked Miss Webster.

"I've had you pointed out to me by just about everyone I've met in town since taking this job," said Mr. Pettinger.

"How funny. Why? Do your children go to Green-willow?" asked Miss Webster.

"Me? No, I'm not married," said Mr. Pettinger, turning pink and changing the subject. "I've room in the truck for whoever wants to come. It might make you feel better to see the nice woods this bear's going to."

Ashley said she didn't want to but Miss Webster and Charlie said they would so it was agreed that Mr. Pettinger would drop Ashley off at her house on their way out of town.

"What about Al?" asked Marlin, digging her elbow into Fiona's ribs. "Do we still give him cookies?"

Fiona thought about it. "I'll take them over anyway with his dinner and tell him he's not needed. He never showed up so he probably didn't even remember that he was supposed to drive her," she said. "We can tell him it's credit for a favor in the future."

In less time than Charlie expected, the bear was safely loaded and then they were off.

Fiona, watching them drive away, felt weak in the knees from the excitement so she ate one of Al's cookies on the way over to his house. One less cookie wouldn't make a difference, she decided. Nor would two.

When she told Al about the whole episode he looked upset. He stood staring dully down the road as she handed him his cookies. He didn't seem to notice them in his hands.

"So Billy's gone for good, I guess," he said flatly.

"Yep," she said, handing him his dinner too. "And since you didn't have to drive Ashley home we thought the cookies could be credit for something in the future."

"Conservation officer," said Al, and spat at the ground. "That bear never did a lick of harm to anyone."

Before Fiona could reply he had gone back in and slammed his door.

Well, it's not my fault, thought Fiona, stomping angrily home. *Does he want the bear to actually eat someone before we call the conservation officer?*

Charlie didn't get back until after the girls had had dinner and it was almost dark. Mr. Pettinger dropped Charlie and Miss Webster where she'd left her car at the side of the house. Miss Webster said a quick good-bye and before Fiona could say no, Charlie had grabbed the bike.

"I just want to tell Al where Billy went," she called over her shoulder. "He's going to be worried."

When Charlie came back she looked subdued.

"Did he yell at you?" asked Marlin finally when Charlie had come in but offered no information.

"No. I told him there's a river where we took Billy with a lot of salmon and Mr. Pettinger said Billy could fish there and would like that. But Al said what Billy really liked were Oreo cookies. He said it's against the law to put food out for bears but he always put some cookies out for Billy anyway on garbage day."

"What else did you talk about?" asked Fiona. "I almost

came to get you, you know you shouldn't be out when it's getting dark."

"Mostly we didn't talk about anything," said Charlie. "We just sat together and looked at two empty garbage cans still on the road and later I told him I saw Billy dancing one night and he said that he's seen him do that too but he didn't know what it was or what Billy was thinking when he did it. That animals may have a whole lot of thoughts and reasons that humans never experience and cannot know. Just as there may be all kinds of colors that no one has ever seen. That the number of things humans don't know is stagging."

"Staggering," corrected Fiona absently.

"He said the animals probably don't know why we do anything either. Why we put garbage out but they can't have it. We can't tell each other because we don't speak the same language."

"Science has found out a lot, though," said Natasha matter-of-factly as she joined them at the kitchen table. "We do know a lot about animal language. Did you know that ravens have syntax?"

"What's that?" asked Charlie.

"I forget," said Natasha. "But it's something to do with language and it's way more sophisticated than you'd think."

"I told Al that you can't know what bears are thinking and he said I was right. Then he said you can't really know anyone. That most people don't even know themselves. He said he thought he knew Martha, though. If there was one person he knew it was her. He moved where he is to be by her and he said she and Billy were the two real friends he'd had in life and now they were both gone."

"Didn't he bark at you at *all*?" asked Marlin, who sat down at the table and passed a plate of the cookies left from the batch she'd made Al.

"No, I think he was too sad to bark."

"And he wasn't mad at you for getting Billy relocated?" asked Fiona, thinking Al hadn't been too sad to bark at *her*.

"Well, he said I was the only one he could talk to about Billy. I was the only one who understood."

"Do you want dinner? I can heat some up in the microwave," said Marlin.

But Charlie said, "Mr. Pettinger treated me and Miss Webster to McDonald's on the way home. She said thanks and he said it wasn't much but he had to get back to his office and turn in a report on the bear but to make up for it could he take her out to a good restaurant tomorrow. But he didn't ask me. Mom always said if you're inviting someone in front of anyone else you have to invite that person too." Charlie looked indignant.

"Of course he didn't invite you, you dingbat," said Marlin. "He was asking her on a date. Did she say yes?"

"Oh yeah, she seemed to be really happy about it," said Charlie. "They talked all the way home. I think they forgot

I was there. She seemed to really like him and I like him too. He'd only just met Billy but he was really nice to him and wanted to make sure he'd be happy."

"Well, conservation officers *become* conservation officers because they love animals, I guess," said Natasha. "I'm thinking of becoming one when I grow up if I don't become an ornithologist only I'm not sure you can do that for a living."

"And what about Ashley's mom? Did she seem upset when you dropped off Ashley in a truck with a bear in tow?" asked Fiona.

"No, she just said, goodness, what a lot of excitement. And thank goodness Miss Webster was a family friend and on hand because Miss Webster lied to her too."

"It's not a lie, she is a family friend," said Marlin.

And thank heavens for that, thought Fiona, who had been on tenterhooks about the visit and what disastrous results it might have.

Later that night when Fiona and Marlin were lying in bed doing their usual end-of-the-day postmortem, Marlin said, "Wouldn't it be cool if Miss Webster and Mr. Pettinger fell in love? He's really handsome, didn't you think?"

"Yeah, I guess," said Fiona, but she wasn't thinking of how handsome Mr. Pettinger was. She had another handsome face in her mind's eye those days. For Fiona had met a boy.

Lost

FIONA had seen him first at lunch. He wasn't in her class because he was a grade ahead of her. He was about the same height as her with a slight build and dark hair, a lock of which fell forward over one eye. He was constantly brushing it back, revealing merry, slightly skeptical eyes. Fiona had noticed him hanging out talking to other kids and without knowing anything about him had felt an unexplainable excitement. Just the sight of him revved her engines a little faster. She'd had crushes on TV and movie stars but he was the first real boy she'd ever felt this way about. She became shy whenever he was near, terrified he would notice her noticing him. She turned her back on him in the school yard and looked the other way at lunch if she spied him. What he looked mostly was smart. Smart, she knew suddenly, was what made her knees go to jelly. But not just any kind of smart. There were lots of ways to be smart. What you wanted was smart in a certain way. Smart that answered to your smart. She told no one about her feelings.

One day at lunch one of the girls she regularly ate with nudged her and said, "Davy Clement is looking at you."

Fiona turned to see who that was and it was the boy. When he tried to catch her eye she turned swiftly back to her friend and said, "No, he's just looking across the room," and changed the subject.

But soon he was all she could think about. She longed for a best friend in whom she could confide. To dissect every look he gave her, to strategize a plan of some sort for meeting him. But to form that kind of friendship meant the friend would have to find out about so many other things—that they were living with no adult taking care of them. That she was caring for her sisters. Maybe in time, in a year or two, she could develop the type of bond where such a person might be trusted. But it was still too soon for that. And she couldn't mention Davy to the girls she had casual friendships with because it might get back to him that she was asking about him. So she kept it, as she now kept so many things, bottled up. At night she would gaze out their bedroom window at the Big Dipper and think about him and what it would be like to hold his hand. To walk with his arm around her waist the way she saw kids in the older grades doing.

Sometimes he seemed to be watching and she thought maybe he wanted these things too but that, she decided, was probably wishful thinking.

Most of the kids at school weren't paired up, they

ran together in packs made up of both boys and girls, all friendly and used to doing things together. Fiona didn't have a pack, she had friends she met for lunch and girls she talked to before and after school but no group she felt she belonged to. She stayed as buttoned-up as she could anyway, keeping conversations short so that they could never work around to anything very personal.

Davy didn't seem to have a pack either. She saw him talking to other kids but often she spotted him on his own. As far as she could tell he never hung out with just one group.

She imagined she saw in him from afar all kinds of good traits. That he was kind and funny and smart and she decided that if she could tell anyone about their living situation it was him. He would keep the secret and would understand. Fiona longed for this. All the strain of their survival was on her shoulders 24-7 and it would be such a relief, such a blessed relief, just to be able to talk about it. She didn't need anyone to help out, she had Miss Webster for emergencies and Al for camouflage, she just needed to be able to pour out all the anxious worries that kept her up nights. The things that twisted through her mind all day long.

While Fiona engaged in her quiet secret romance, the town of St. Mary's By the Sea was buzzing with the real and concrete romance of Donald Pettinger and Miss Webster. They were now dating quite publicly and his truck was often in the school parking lot either dropping her off in the morning or waiting for her after school. Charlie was particularly thrilled by this because she felt responsible.

"If I hadn't been stuck in a tree with Billy Bear, they might never have met," she said at dinner one night.

"They probably would have met eventually," said Marlin. "From what he said, everyone in town seemed to be pushing her at him. And she must be really serious about him or she would never have told him our secret."

"What would she have told him?" asked Natasha.

"I don't know but she's an inveterate liar," said Marlin. "So it would have been good. Look how she handled Ashley's mom."

"I hope you're right," said Fiona. "Because if they break up, it's one more person who knows about us but now one who hasn't a loyal stake in keeping our secret."

"He would never tell anyone," said Charlie.

"Besides, maybe they'll marry," said Marlin. "He's the most handsome bachelor in St. Mary's By the Sea and she's the prettiest bachelorette."

"I think that's shallow," said Natasha. "You shouldn't choose a mate based on looks. Although there are birds…"

"We're not talking about birds," said Marlin.

"If they get married, they can adopt us," said Charlie.

"Charlie," warned Fiona. "Don't say that around Miss Webster. Ever. Or Mr. Pettinger."

"I wouldn't but I bet they're thinking it. They seem to like us a lot," Charlie went on happily. "Of everyone in town they're the ones I choose."

"Well, yes," said Fiona. "They'd make kind of ideal guardians. But we don't get to choose and besides, there isn't the slightest hint of that, so don't even think it."

"And last Sunday," Charlie went on as if Fiona hadn't said anything, "they sat on the back steps and she said that of everywhere she's lived in the world she loves Pine Island the best and she'd love to have a little farm just like ours. She'd keep horses and some sheep."

"And he said he wanted that too. With a couple of dogs thrown in," said Natasha.

"They could move right in!" said Charlie.

"Where would we put them? I don't want to move our beds back in with you small fry," said Marlin.

"He could build another bedroom onto the side of the house for them," said Charlie. "He can do anything."

Fiona had been privately thinking about possible arrangements like this herself. Miss Webster and Mr. Pettinger had taken to coming over every Sunday for what had long ceased to be Miss Webster's inspection and become her pleasure and they always stayed for dinner. Mr. Pettinger had wanted the girls to call him Don but Miss Webster said they had to continue to call her Miss Webster so they wouldn't accidentally slip at school and address her as Diana. That made sense to everyone and the girls decided to keep calling him Mr. Pettinger for the symmetry, as Marlin put it.

On Sundays they would all hang out at the farm, playing card and board games that Mr. Pettinger bought for them. He seemed very fond of Monopoly and Yahtzee and the games became very animated with lots of shouting and laughter. The girls had never played board games with shouting and they found it added an exciting component.

Marlin tried out the fanciest recipes she could find for their Sunday dinners. Mr. Pettinger said he couldn't possibly cadge dinner without paying them back so whenever he came over he fixed whatever needed fixing, leaky pipes, hanging gutters, broken screens, and once when he caught Natasha sitting on a kitchen chair at the living room window watching the birds, he brought over some lumber and built them a window seat, which Miss Webster covered in a bench cushion she made herself with a fabric arrayed in bluebirds.

"For happiness," she said as she laid the cushion down and they all exclaimed over it. "Against all odds this is the happiest place I can ever remember being."

Fiona knew part of Miss Webster's happiness stemmed from the fact that Mr. Pettinger was there. But it was also true that despite all odds, there was a peace that seemed generated from the farm, as if it existed deep in the soil and emanated upward. Perhaps it was the quality of the quiet; the sounds that they heard there were all peaceful sounds. She might be anxious about their continuing welfare but there was a lovely, slow elegance to these spring days, fragrant with fruit blossoms and sunbaked pine needles. Every morning she woke to the joyful sound of birds announcing the sunrise and every night she fell asleep to the mad chirping of the tree frogs, sounding the plea for mates. It was as regular and right as the rising and setting of the sun and moon. Or the ingoing, outgoing rhythm of the tides. And if Miss Webster and Mr. Pettinger would only hurry and marry and adopt them, they would never have to worry again. And even if they didn't, their happiness as they were now was an unexpected state of being.

Her mother was wrong, thought Fiona, feeling disloyal even as she thought it, but she did. You can be both joyful and fearful. You can be in awed peace and suffer at the same time. You can have all things happening at once. It doesn't need to be one or the other. In fact, knowing she could have both at once made Fiona feel like she could breathe. She didn't have to strain for the joyful. She didn't have to kick out the fearful. She could just greet the day as it was.

After Mr. Pettinger built the window seat and the girls had expressed surprise at his carpentry skills he said that he had grown up in a cabin in the Yukon, a hundred miles from anyone else, and if you didn't know how to do something yourself you had to learn fast. He and his brothers and sisters could do all kinds of things, carpentry, plumbing, fishing, trapping, farming. Sometimes the girls would hang out with him while he fixed something and then he would insist on teaching them how to do it.

"You should learn as many things like this as you can. You never know when it will come in handy," he said to Natasha one day as they caulked the tub.

"But we can just call you," she said.

"It's always better if you know how to do things yourself," he said. "You need to be your own backup plan."

But Natasha scoffed at the idea of being her own backup plan. She wanted Miss Webster and Mr. Pettinger as their backup plan.

That night after they had gone home she said to her sisters, "See, they would be perfect on the farm. Maybe Miss Webster wouldn't even *want* to be a principal anymore. She could be a farmer."

"What if they want their own children?" asked Fiona. "Most people do."

"Their children could live here too," said Charlie.

"Yes," said Fiona, laughing. "I wasn't suggesting they send them away. But where?"

"He could just keep building bedrooms," said Charlie.

"And they'd have us for babysitters!" said Marlin. "It would be kind of ideal for them, I would think."

"We could get horses!" said Natasha.

Everyone thought it was a wonderful plan.

"But we will not mention it," warned Fiona repeatedly. "Not once. Not to anyone. If it happens, let it be their idea."

"What about Al then?" asked Charlie. "Won't his feelings get hurt?"

"I doubt it," said Fiona. "I doubt he *has* feelings. He only agreed to pretend to be our guardian for the money. He wasn't going to do it at all until we offered to pay him. And I wouldn't mind having that eighty bucks a month back if we do get adopted by someone else."

"Is money low?" asked Marlin.

"We have enough," said Fiona. "But it won't last forever. We're good for this year and the one after."

Maybe, she wanted to add because there were even more expenses and complications than she had counted on when she had originally totted up what they had and what it would take to live. She now knew there were taxes and insurance as well as the utilities and the expensive phone plan and internet. She was beginning to get letters from Hiram Pennypacker. He was furious that Al had not come in with proof of guardianship. He wanted her to come in to talk about taxes. He wanted her to sign things. At first he sent requests by snail mail in a formal lawyerlike fashion. Then he sent her emails and texts and finally he began phoning. She let all his phone calls go to voice mail. She ignored his emails and texts and she buried his letters at the bottom of her underwear drawer.

If she could just avoid him, she thought, until she could figure out what to do about the legal guardianship, then he wouldn't accidentally find out what was going on. She knew this was lame but she had enough to do with her schoolwork, overseeing Marlin, Natasha, and Charlie, and keeping the house running. She thought she was doing a pretty good job keeping it going smoothly and that the family's needs and wants were mostly provided for. Then one day after school Natasha said she wanted to join strings.

"Strings?" said Fiona.

"Yeah, you can rent a violin from the school and you learn how to play it and you play it in this string group. My teacher said they are asking for people to sign up now for next fall so they know how many people are going to be in it."

She handed Fiona the notice. Fiona read it. There was the violin rental and the lessons, which students had to take privately in order to belong to the strings group. Fiona looked at the final estimated cost.

"We can't afford it," she said flatly.

Natasha looked astonished. "But you said we had money," she said.

"We have money for necessities. This isn't a necessity, Nat."

Natasha's face fell. Then, as was her way, she didn't argue, she just put her school things down, picked up her binoculars, and went out to the backyard to watch birds.

Fiona felt the way you do after you've had to rip a particularly painful Band-Aid off someone. She gave a sigh. Marlin would have been angry. Charlie would have cried. It hurt the most to say no to Natasha. She sucked things up and moved back into her own quiet little world where she drifted most times, watching wildlife, keeping track of birds, going off alone to sit on the beach, lost in thoughts she never shared. The only time Fiona got angry with her parents for dying was when she was worried about Nat. There was something different about Natasha. Fiona and Marlin and Charlie all caused their share of worry but even though Charlie was fearful, even though Fiona sometimes wondered if Charlie needed help dealing with her fears, Fiona always knew in the end Charlie would be okay. But she was never sure this way about Natasha. There were parts of her that were so unreachable that Fiona worried that if Natasha crawled back into that part of herself, she would disappear and no one would be able to retrieve her. The heartbreaking vulnerability of Nat had been her parents' problem. Natasha should have *stayed* their problem. She had always worried about Natasha a little as her sister but her parents had had the brunt of the worry. Now it was Fiona's alone.

But she couldn't dwell on Natasha's disappointment, she had laundry loads to do, and an English paper to write, and then it was her turn to take dinner to Al. It was almost dinner when she realized she hadn't seen Nat all afternoon and she was supposed to do her homework before supper. They all did their homework before supper so that they could watch TV together afterward. It was like Nat to forget, though, if not reminded.

Fiona looked out back and couldn't see her so she went onto the back porch and called. There was no answer. Was Nat angrier than Fiona had expected? Just because Fiona had said no to strings? Had she run off to hide? But that wasn't like Nat. Natasha knew she and Charlie were not supposed to disappear on them. It was one of the few hard rules Fiona had made. They must always be in shouting distance because Fiona had enough to worry about without rounding them all up for dinner or worrying where they'd gone. She called again but still no Natasha so Fiona went down the beach trail. Perhaps she'd followed a bird down there. She had her binoculars and the surf could be loud when the tide was going in or out. Nat might not have heard her calling.

But when she got down to the beach the tide was in and there was only a little pebbly beach left, not enough to be pleasant for sitting, and there was no sign of Nat anyway. She called over and over just in case but her calls were only met with seagull cries and the sound of waves. She turned and scurried back up to the meadow calling all the way to the house in increasing volume and concern. This brought Marlin, who had been putting the finishing touches on dinner. And Charlie, who swiftly joined them.

"Do you know where Natasha went?" Fiona asked. "She left with her binoculars a long time ago and now she's not answering."

Both Marlin and Charlie looked upset. They knew none of them would cause this kind of worry on purpose.

"She must be lost," said Marlin, voicing what none of them had wanted to. And if any one of them was going to get lost in the hundreds of miles of forest that extended from their property it was most apt to be Natasha, who drifted about dreamily paying little attention to her surroundings.

"We have to get help," said Fiona, panicking in earnest now. She was suddenly filled with terror at all the dangers surrounding them. The canopy of the forest was so thick that if Search and Rescue sent choppers to look for someone they could never find them from above through the density of trees. And the ocean was never safe. You could fall from one of the cliffs, hit your head, and be pulled out by a rip and no one would ever find out what had happened to you. You could be standing on what you thought was a safe rocky promontory and a rogue wave could come suddenly barreling in, lifting you and taking you back with it before you even saw it coming. Fiona had heard friends at school talk about losing a tourist every year this way. And Billy Bear wasn't the only bear in those forests. There were more malevolent bears, not to mention cougars and wolves.

"Call Miss Webster," said Charlie.

"Right," said Fiona, hurrying for the phone.

Miss Webster answered and as soon as she heard Fiona's voice said, "What's wrong?"

Fiona explained and Miss Webster said calmly and decidedly, "Okay, don't any of you go out into the woods after her. We don't need all of you lost. You sit tight at the house. Keep calling her name if you need to but go nowhere. I'm going to organize a search. I'm going to call Don too. And we'll call Search and Rescue if we need to. Chances are she isn't far from the house."

They hung up. Fiona paced and then something occurred to her. "I'm going to Al's," she said.

"Oh, who cares about his dinner at a time like this," said Marlin.

"No, we need him here. If the house is swarming with people asking questions he'd better be on-site too. We don't need people asking why there wasn't an adult here when Natasha went missing."

Fiona ran over to Al's trailer half hoping that although she'd never done it before, Natasha had gone there for some reason of her own. But when Al answered the door expecting his supper, she charged in breathless and said, "Is Natasha here?"

"What? What?" he said in confusion.

"NATASHA! She left with her binoculars and she hasn't come back. We think she's lost in the woods."

"Oh no," said Al, and sat down on the couch.

"And we need you to come over. Our principal, Miss Webster, is bringing people to help search and we are worried questions will be asked. You have to come over and pretend to live with us."

Al nodded and put on his shoes. Then they started out the door and down the road. But he could not keep up with Fiona, who was practically running while he stumbled, none too steady on his feet.

Oh, great, she thought. *People are going to find us with a grown-up but a drunk one.*

But this was such a small worry compared to Natasha's disappearance that she gave it no more thought and began to call Natasha's name again.

People arrived constantly after that. Miss Webster and Mr. Pettinger were the first but slowly people they didn't even know were pulling up in cars. The whole of the girls' driveway and both sides of the road were lined with the cars of people who had heard about the lost little girl. Finally, Miss Webster decided it was time to call the volunteer fire department, Search and Rescue, and the police, all of whom arrived almost immediately after being phoned. Al did his part pretending to be the official spokesperson although Fiona caught one officer making a face of disgust as he smelled the beer on Al's breath. But at such a time no one was going to say anything admonishing to anyone. One Search and Rescue worker even patted Al reassuringly on the arm and said he was sure they'd find Natasha, not to worry.

But two hours passed and Natasha had still not been found. Then began a steady drenching West Coast rain. Searchers came into the house to warm up, telling the girls not to panic, Natasha wasn't the first person lost in the woods. They were always found. Everyone seemed to have a story about an aunt or cousin or friend who went missing for two days, six days, a month, and returned alive. Fiona found some comfort in these stories and the kindness of the people telling them. It kept her hopeful between bouts of wondering where in the world Nat could be and the niggling thought, *Yes, your cousin returned but that doesn't mean it will be the case this time.*

People searched until they were drenched and then they drove home to change and return. Others arrived with food and put it on tables and counters all over the house. One woman brought a large coffee urn from the community hall and kept it full. All that the girls could hear from the house, from which they were not allowed to stray, was Natasha's name being yelled over and over through the woods and up the sides of mountains that made the backdrop of the property. To Fiona it was the terrible silence it was met with that was the worst. Not to be able to imagine what had befallen Natasha or where she was or why she was not answering. Not knowing if something terrible had already happened to her. To hear her name and the following silence like the silence of her parents after their death. They might call to them too but there would never again be an answer.

Fiona paced and could not stop this exhausting movement back and forth across the room, not even to reassure Charlie. After the fourth hour there was nothing anyone could say that would reassure her. Where was Natasha? Where *was* she? With so many people screaming for her, why could she not hear them? Why had she not yet been found?

Occasionally a grown-up would come in and say something to Al. At one point Hiram Pennypacker had shown up in blue jeans to help search and gave Al a hard stare as if to say, this is all your fault. You were supposed to be watching them. But no one could voice blame at such a time with such terrible thoughts of what still might be.

It was ten-thirty at night and pitch dark when Fiona, who had been stiff-lipped until then, began to cry. Al had sobered up by then and wanted to join the search but Search and Rescue said they wanted the girls' guardian in the house with the girls just in case. It was this "just in case" that triggered Fiona. And once she started crying she couldn't stop. Marlin looked terrified by Fiona's tears and Charlie was stiff as a board, hardly breathing, sitting in a corner of the living room, speaking to no one, not even the kind women who came and tried to distract her with a storybook. Finally, as the realization sank in that the search might go on all night and crews would be heading further into the woods and the hardware store owner had just volunteered to go for more outdoor lanterns and powerful flashlights from his stock, Mr. Pettinger came down off the mountain with Natasha's shaking and soaked-to-the-bone body in his arms.

"NAT!" cried Fiona, running out of the house, slipping in the meadow and getting coated in mud but not even noticing as she sprang up again and ran forward.

After that the volunteer fire department called the fire hall and had the siren turned on, the Search and Rescue signal to everyone that Natasha had been found. People started coming slowly back out of the woods, wet and chilled and anxious to hear if she was unharmed.

"I found her halfway up the other side of the mountain shivering under a tree," said Mr. Pettinger, whose arms were shaking with the fatigue of carrying her.

The paramedics who had been on hand checked her over and declared she wasn't hypothermic, just cold and wet and exhausted, and she should have a hot bath, a hot drink, and bed. Miss Webster oversaw this while people slowly drifted away, taking their empty casserole dishes and plates and the coffee urn with them. No one quizzed the girls. Everyone seemed to understand that what they needed was quiet. Even the police and Search and Rescue packed up quietly with no further ado. Finally Miss Webster, who was helping Marlin do the dishes, asked the girls if they wanted her to stay the night. She did this without thinking because Mr. Pennypacker was standing right by and a light seemed to go on behind his eyes.

"Why would you stay the night?" he asked maliciously as if he'd finally caught them out. "Al's their guardian, isn't he?"

For a split second Miss Webster understood her mistake and froze before she replied as casually as she could, "Oh, but I think sometimes in situations like this a girl misses a mother figure."

"Uh-huh," said Mr. Pennypacker, looking skeptical, and found Al, who was sorting through Martha's books in the living room and said to him, "You haven't even moved in yet, have you? You haven't shown me any paperwork because you haven't *got* any, right? I bet you're nothing to these girls any more than you were to Martha. My only question is why are these girls lying for you?"

Noooo, thought Fiona, who had heard this exchange, *nooooo.* But she was too exhausted to deal with yet another crisis. She heard Mr. Pennypacker follow Al outside to the porch but she could only pick up bits and pieces of what he said, mostly it was, "You're not, are you? You've all been lying to me. I'll tell you why, because she would never have put you in charge of anything. She knew what you were."

Al answered but his answers and Mr. Pennypacker's further inquiries became impossible to distinguish and finally their voices stopped as Mr. Pennypacker's car door slammed and with an angry roar of his engine, he drove off. She peered out the window and saw Al head home.

Outed, thought Fiona grimly. *Now what?*

After that she was busy saying good-bye to Miss Webster and Mr. Pettinger, who stood at the front door with their arms around each other.

"All's well that ends well, huh?" he said to Fiona.

Fiona knew he was trying to buck her up but she wanted to say, if you want this to end well you'd better hurry up and marry Miss Webster and adopt us because I don't think Mr. Pennypacker is going to sit on these increasing suspicions for long. But she said nothing. She was numb with fatigue and the aftermath of worry so she just nodded.

Once it was just the four of them, Fiona went upstairs with the others to hear Natasha's story. They'd been too busy clearing people out and Natasha had been too busy trying to warm up and recover to talk. Even now she was almost asleep and not terribly coherent.

"I went out to follow eagles. I just wanted to see where they nested. I know they have a nest somewhere in the back forest because I see them always returning there. I started going and I thought, *I can just backtrack the way I came* and then I kept backtracking but the bushes grew thicker. So then I'd turn around and no matter which way I went I couldn't find our farm. When I knew I was lost I kept thinking, *Well, I'll just head downhill, if I go down then I'll end up at the ocean and can follow the cliffs home.* But I went down and then there was nothing there but another hill so I'd go up and then before I knew it I was really lost."

"Didn't you hear me call?" asked Fiona.

"Yes, a few times so I'd head in that direction and I called back but you never answered."

"I didn't hear you, Nat," said Fiona. "Did you hear everyone else calling? Did you call back?"

"No, I didn't hear anything after I stopped hearing you and I just kept going hoping to hear your voice again but I guess I went in the wrong direction and then the wind and rain started and I got really scared because I was getting so wet and the trees were creaking like they were going to fall on me. And then I got tired and I was wet and cold and I didn't know why you didn't hear me and call back when I called and I was afraid to keep going, that I was going even further away, so I just sat under a tree waiting for her."

"For us, Nat?"

"No," whispered Nat. "For Mommy." And she fell asleep.

"It would have happened even if Mommy and Daddy had been alive," said Marlin to Fiona later after Charlie had fallen asleep too and the two of them had retired to their own beds to stare at the ceiling.

"I know," said Fiona wretchedly.

"She's always drifting off without paying attention. It could have happened in Borneo just as easily. But that Al Farber is a waste of space. Did you see he was drunk when he got here?"

"We need a better pretend guardian," mumbled Fiona because she had already shut her eyes, which were growing too heavy to keep open.

Through her half-awake state she heard Marlin say, "It's so weird."

"What's so weird," asked Fiona, yawning.

"That Mommy and Daddy will never know we came to Pine Island. That they'll never know Natasha was lost. That they'll never know anything that happens to us from now on."

Davy Clement

THE air grew lighter, the days lengthened, and they entered May, the most glorious of months. The letters, emails, texts, and phone calls from Mr. Pennypacker stopped. Fiona did not know if this was a good thing or a bad thing until one day when she took Al's dinner over he said, "You gotta get that annoying limpet Hiram Pennypacker off my back."

Fiona paled. "What do you mean?"

"I mean he's constantly leaving me threatening messages. He says it's only because of his loyalty to Martha and the chance that she really did want me as the guardian that he hasn't gone to social services yet. But it's the same message on my phone every day, over and over in his annoying high-pitched little squeak. I can't make him stop, I can't even call him back, because I have no paperwork to show him and there's not a reason I can think of that he would believe for not showing it to him if I had it!"

"Oh," said Fiona.

"Yeah, *oh,*" said Al. "Whatever I signed up for it wasn't being nagged to death by that garden gnome."

"Don't worry," said Fiona, thinking of Miss Webster and Mr. Pettinger. She needed so desperately for them to come to their rescue that she now believed the adoption fantasy implicitly. "We have a backup plan. You may not have to pretend to be our guardian much longer."

"Really?" said Al, looking intrigued. "What's happening?"

"Never mind. It's confidential for now. But I promise you, if things go as we think they might, we can get Mr. Pennypacker off your back completely. You just have to hang on a bit. In the meantime, do what I do and ignore him."

Al rolled his eyes, took his dinner into the trailer, and slammed the door.

He still had little time for any of them except Charlie. He had started picking Charlie up on Saturdays with a box of Oreos and they drove to the Salmon River trail to look for Billy Bear.

Fiona was admonishing Charlie about this one night at Sunday night supper with Miss Webster and Mr. Pettinger.

"You know that's dangerous, don't you?" she said.

"If you want to look for Billy Bear, you should let me take you," said Mr. Pettinger.

"But Al and I like to go together," said Charlie. "Besides, mostly we sit in the truck watching for him. We haven't seen him yet but we always leave a little cairn of Oreos for him when we leave."

"A cairn?" said Natasha.

"It's a rock pile people build," said Charlie. "Only Al makes it out of Oreos. He calls it the bear cairn of cookies."

"You're not supposed to do that," said Mr. Pettinger. "A fed bear is a dead bear."

"Al fed him when he lived in our woods," said Charlie. "Al always left him Oreos on garbage day."

"Yes, and that's why he had to be moved. At least in part. I know Billy was into the garbage but the cookies couldn't have helped. If he gets used to people giving him food up there in the woods then when he sees people he's going to come toward them looking for food and that's how you end up with a dead bear."

"Well, we don't hand him anything because he's never there," said Charlie. "We just sit and eat cookies and look for him and then leave him a snack for later."

"Even if Billy doesn't connect people with the cookies you leave, you shouldn't do it," insisted Mr. Pettinger. "For one thing, Oreos are not healthy food."

"*We* eat them," pointed out Charlie.

"What do you talk about?" asked Marlin, changing the subject. "When I bring Al his dinner all he does is yell 'WHAT!' and then take it and give me the empty food container from the night before."

"We don't talk about anything," said Charlie. "Well, sometimes about how we miss Billy. That's all."

"Does he talk about Aunt Martha?" asked Fiona.

"Or what it was like to write for the *New York Times*?" asked Marlin.

"Nope," said Charlie. "I asked him once what Aunt Martha was like and he said, read the book. So then I asked him what it was like to be a writer and he said, read the book. Then I asked him why he'd never written another book and he said, none of your business."

"Jeez, does he always have to be so *sour*?" said Marlin.

"I like him," said Charlie. "He says what he thinks and he never makes me nervous."

Fiona was startled by this comment. Did the rest of them make Charlie nervous? Did she? Did she hover? Part of her was constantly tweaking her job of taking care of all of them. Maybe she was being too nice to Charlie, too solicitous. Maybe she should bark "none of your business" more often. It seemed all she ever did was worry that she was inadequate to the job of keeping them all afloat and that she was doing it all wrong.

But she had one respite from these constant worries. One place she could retreat to in her head. And that was daydreaming about Davy. There was some kind of magical electrical current between them so that she could swear she knew where he was in the school at any time. One day she was sitting idly on one of the tree stumps in the yard in front of the school waiting for the bell to ring when she thought,

He's going to walk around the corner of that building right now and he did. He saw her there, her face full of surprise at her own prescience, and he smiled at her. She was so startled she didn't have time to turn away and there was no one she knew nearby with whom to engage in conversation so she just sat, her mouth slightly open, until he came up.

"Hi," he said.

"Hi," she said back, her face getting hot.

"You're new this year, right? You and your sisters. My little sister is in class with Natasha. She says that you guys came from Borneo."

"Yep," said Fiona.

"Wow," he said. "I just wanted to tell you I thought that was pretty cool. Borneo."

"Thanks," she said, then wanted to give herself a kick as she thought what a stupid thing that was to say. Thanks for what?

"I'm Davy Clement," he said.

"I know," she said, and then wanted to give herself another kick. How would she know unless she had asked about him? "I'm Fiona McCready."

"I know," he said, and smiled again as if they'd made their first joke together. "So what do you think of St. Mary's By the Sea?"

"I haven't seen much of it. Mostly just the grocery store when I do the weekly shopping."

He looked surprised. She was so rattled she was making small and silly mistakes after being careful for weeks. What fourteen-year-old did the grocery shopping for her family every week?

"I like to grocery-shop," she elaborated, hoping that would make it sound more normal. "So that's sort of become my chore."

"That's cool that your parents let you," he said.

"My parents are dead," said Fiona flatly. She still had trouble saying it so baldly, as if by saying it, she lowered the coffins. There had been no bodies to bury so her parents' death remained in many ways abstract. Something that could be changed, even though she knew better. Stating aloud that they were dead felt disloyal. It seemed like a willingness to kill that small barely discernable hope.

"Wow," said Davy. "Who do you live with?"

"Oh, we have a legal guardian named Al Farber," she said. "We were going to live with my great-aunt Martha but she died too."

"That's a...you must...how long ago did your parents die?"

"Well, it's been over a year. So it's not, you know, fresh."

"Still, I guess you don't really get used to it."

"No. Well, you sort of do and sort of don't."

He nodded. "Was it a car accident or something?"

"Tsunami."

"Wow. That one in Thailand?"

"Yeah."

"Wow. I saw that on the news. That's horrible."

"Yeah, pretty much."

"Well, I was just going to ask you if you wanted to walk into town after school today and I could show you where the Fudge Fairy has her stand. That's what she calls herself. She's been around forever. She makes fudge and bow ties for a living. I thought you might not have found it yet yourself. It's kind of tucked away on a back street. She makes a hundred and twenty-two kinds of fudge, not all at once, but she has that many flavors concocted and she rotates them. She usually has about a dozen kinds on the stand. It's the best fudge you've ever had."

"I can't," Fiona said quickly. "I have to watch my sisters after school."

"Oh," said Davy, looking embarrassed as if he'd taken a chance and now found he had read her wrong after all. He backed up two steps. "Does your guardian work or something and so you do the after-school care?"

"Yeah, sort of."

"Okay, well, no problem." He took two more steps back, turning slightly to go.

"I really do," she said. "Otherwise I would. I'd like to see the fudge stand. But thanks for asking."

"That's okay," he said, and sauntered off. "Maybe some other day."

"Okay," she said, but she said it quietly because she was thinking, *What other day?*

When would she dare to go off somewhere after school and not worry that someone was going to get treed by a bear or lost in the woods? She should have asked if he wanted to meet when she was in town to do the grocery shopping already. She left the others with Marlin then. Marlin was almost thirteen. Why couldn't Marlin watch Natasha and Charlie after school if she could watch them on Saturdays? Why hadn't she thought of *that*?

"Some other day," she muttered again hopefully but he was out of earshot.

After that she didn't see him for a while. She didn't know if he saw her and avoided her or if it was just happenstance that they weren't running into each other as much.

She had other things to think about anyway. Something was going on with both Marlin and Miss Webster. She didn't know if the two things were connected but they both went around with the same air of suppressed excitement.

One day at supper Fiona said, "What is going on with you, Marlin?"

"I have a secret," said Marlin. "But I don't want to tell you yet."

"Is it the same secret that Miss Webster has?" asked

Fiona. "Because she comes over now looking like she's going to burst. What's going on with the two of you?"

"Miss Webster?" said Marlin. "What kind of secret would I have with her? No, this is my own."

"Well, give us a clue," said Fiona.

"I think I've found a way to make money so that Nat can go to strings and you don't have to worry so much. But I can't tell you yet."

"I can go to strings?" asked Natasha, looking up suddenly with interest from her plate of food.

"Is it legal?" asked Fiona.

"Is it *legal*!" said Marlin, indignantly standing up.

"All right, all right, Marlin, it's just I can't imagine how a twelve-year-old could suddenly make a lot of money."

"That's right," said Marlin smugly. "You can't imagine. But I can and I've found a way to solve all our problems."

"Well, that's, that's great," said Fiona warily. She didn't think for a moment that Marlin had found a way to make money. She had no idea what she had up her sleeve, some kind of pipe dream probably but if it made Marlin happy that was fine with her. She wasn't going to worry about it.

Fiona wished she could ask Miss Webster the way she had Marlin why she was going around looking like the cat who swallowed the canary. She was hoping it was because Miss Webster and Mr. Pettinger were planning to adopt them. Al was beginning to threaten her that if they didn't get Mr. Pennypacker off his back their original agreement was over. She didn't feel she could pry into Miss Webster's thoughts the way she could Marlin's but the following Sunday Miss Webster volunteered some information on her own.

Mr. Pettinger was in the orchard hanging a swing for the girls. Miss Webster had brought over an old-fashioned ice cream machine and some rock salt and dry ice and she and the girls were sitting on the porch taking turns cranking it when Miss Webster said, "This is the most beautiful spring I can ever remember. And I have a big beautiful secret to go with it. It comes in two parts. I'm not telling anyone yet. But I will tell you girls first when it's time because it affects the four of you the most. So there you go, that's something fun for you to mull over this week, isn't it?"

"Does that mean you're telling us next weekend?" asked Marlin excitedly.

"Maybe. But probably in another week or two. We're just straightening some details."

Fiona shot Charlie a nervous look, worried that Charlie would burst out with "We know!" or worse, "You're adopting us!" But it was Charlie's turn to crank the ice cream handle and that kept her happily preoccupied.

That evening after Mr. Pettinger and Miss Webster had gone, Marlin said, "A secret with *two* parts!"

"They're adopting us!" said Charlie.

"Miss Webster practically spat it out on the spot!" said Natasha.

"Maybe," said Fiona because even she couldn't help thinking this must surely be the secret and that it was coming not a moment too soon before things got too sticky with Mr. Pennypacker.

"What do you think part one is?" asked Marlin.

"Well, obviously that they're getting married," said Natasha.

"No, that they're adopting us!" said Charlie again.

"Part two?" said Natasha.

"They're buying us all ponies!" said Charlie.

"More likely part one is they're getting married," said Marlin.

"Maybe," said Fiona cautiously. "But, I mean they *just* met. Too soon? And none of us can speculate about this in front of them. *Ever.* We cannot let on what we're hoping for and if it turns out that that *is* the secret, we have to act surprised."

"Good," said Charlie. "We have a secret too. Our secret is that we know *their* secret! But they don't know ours, which is that we know *theirs.*"

"Maybe," said Fiona. "But it's dangerous to assume."

Fiona began to think her own private secret might be over and that Davy would never talk to her again. That she hadn't handled the decline of his invitation well. He obviously felt rebuffed. It had been over a week since they'd last talked. She was an idiot. She had ruined things before they even got started.

Then one day when she was sitting on the stump waiting for the bell he came around the side of the building, spied her, and put one finger up as if to say, wait. Then, grinning, he took off his backpack, opened the back pocket, grabbed something out, came over, and handed it to her.

"Birthday cake confetti," he said. "The best fudge flavor in my opinion."

"This is for me?" she asked.

"Well, if you can't make it to the fudge stand, the fudge can come to you." He looked embarrassed.

The bell rang and she was torn. She wanted to stay and talk and now she had to go in.

"Thanks," she said. "Do you want to meet here for lunch maybe?"

"Stump lunch," he said, grinning again. "Sure."

She was trembling with her own bold invitation. "Okay," she said, and walked quickly into the building to hide her shaky legs.

After that they met every day for lunch. Talking was still awkward. She sometimes thought she spent more time when she was with him worrying about how she was coming off than listening to what he was saying.

She wondered how long she would be able to keep her friendship with him from her sisters and what they would think when they found out. Being in separate schools helped but even so Davy had a sister in Natasha's class and if he told her about their lunches together she might tell Natasha. Or someone else might tell any of her sisters. And because she and Davy had lunch together every day, word was beginning to go around the secondary school.

The girls she normally had lunch with began to tease her about having a boyfriend. She tried to avoid this topic and downplay it, feeling that any fuss she made would only exacerbate the talk. She didn't even know why she didn't want to tell her sisters, even Marlin when they lay every night in side-by-side cots staring out the window at the stars and discussing almost everything else. She puzzled it out and realized that she didn't want to tell them because it was something that was hers alone. The one corner of her life for herself. Nearly everything she did now felt as if she did it for the family. For the survival and continuing union of them. And she did not for a second regret that. But here was a little refuge. A place just for her. A place where she could have feelings of her own that were not for the benefit of others. And part of her might feel a bit guilty too because she had had to say no to her sisters. To the things that they wanted. No to Charlie when she wanted the latest fashion doll. No to Natasha for strings. No to Marlin for some of the fancier cooking ingredients and implements she would like to buy. No, no, no. It felt so unfair that she herself had something special that made her happy. Something she didn't have to ask for. Something that had nothing to do with the rest of them. Something of her own. But then it was something that cost them nothing.

More and more Fiona was worried about money. She had recently gotten an email from Hiram Pennypacker with the subject line TAXES!!!!!!! She had ignored it as long as she could but now she pulled it up and found she had ignored it too long. It turned out they owed taxes on complicated things because of their inheritance, things that made her head spin like the difference between the value of Martha's house when she had bought it and what it had recently been assessed at. These taxes and others were past the due date so there would be penalties.

All of this Mr. Pennypacker had tried to warn her about and the reason she had checked his email at all was that one night when it was her turn to bring Al his dinner he had met her at the door with, "DO. YOUR. TAXES! Do your taxes and get that garden gnome off my back. He seems to think as your guardian I should be doing them. Which is ironic since he doesn't believe I *am* your guardian and by the way, that has to be resolved. He's not going to let this go on forever. But right now, TAXES!"

"All right," said Fiona. "I'll look into it."

"Don't look into it. Do them."

So Fiona found the forms online. She had their banking information. The taxes came with instructions. There was even tax software she could buy. She figured she could handle it but when Marlin came in one night she found Fiona silently weeping over them.

"Do you want me to try?" asked Marlin.

"Ha! I wish," sobbed Fiona. "Why do they make it so hard?"

"Can't we hire someone to do them?" asked Marlin.

"No. We can't afford it," said Fiona, using the phrase she was by now so sick of. She felt like she used it every day. And she wondered when would come the day that she had to use it for groceries. *Do not borrow trouble,* she heard her mother's voice in her head.

＊＊＊＊＊＊

She began to keep a notebook of all her parents' favorite phrases for bucking the girls up. Surely there was help there somewhere. Don't borrow trouble. Always look on the bright side. A stitch in time saves nine. The world is so full of a number of things, I'm sure we should all be as happy as kings. But every night she still came home to the unconquerable taxes, which always ended in tears of frustration.

One day when she took Al's dinner over to him, instead

of grabbing it from her and shutting the door as he usually did he said, "Marlin says you can't do the taxes."

"I'm still trying," said Fiona patiently, thinking, *What do you care?*

"Give 'em," he said in his characteristic brusque way.

"What do you mean?"

"Bring 'em over."

"It's all online. I'm using Martha's computer."

"All right. I'll come over there."

Fiona didn't know what to think. Al had never done anything without expecting something in return. All the way back to their house she wondered what it was he wanted but she couldn't imagine. *Don't look a gift horse in the mouth* popped into her head from her parents' lexicon. So she set him up quietly in her aunt's office with Martha's computer, their banking information, and the partially filled-out forms. He was still working on them and eating the pie out of his dinner container when she went to bed.

"Why is he doing it?" she whispered to Marlin.

"Perhaps out of the goodness of his heart," said Marlin. "He must do *some* things just out of the goodness of his heart."

"He never has up till now."

"Maybe he's going to demand three meals a day in return," said Marlin.

"He would have asked for it up front. He likes to

negotiate, I think. Why did you tell him I was having trouble anyway?"

"I don't know. It just slipped out. Because he was nagging me to nag you about the taxes because Mr. Pennypacker was on his case and he was saying how Mr. Pennypacker, or that garden gnome as he calls him, wasn't part of the original agreement and if you didn't get him off his back soon the deal was off and blah blah blah and I just blurted out, 'Well, she's doing the best she can. She's sobbing over them every night as it is.'"

"Oh," said Fiona. "That's probably why then. He probably wants to keep Mr. Pennypacker off his back and figures it's faster in the long run to do the taxes himself."

"Do you think he can do them, though?" asked Marlin. "I mean he seems pretty out of it most of the time. How much longer do you think he'll be down there? Do you think we can just fall asleep before he's gone? Is that rude? Should we stay up to see him to the door the way Mom did with guests?"

"Well, he can't be any worse at it than I was. And I'm too tired to stay up any longer, I don't care if it *is* rude," said Fiona wearily, and fell asleep.

When she got up the next morning she found a note from Al saying, *I printed them out. Sign where I left the Post-it and send a check. P.S. It wasn't really all that hard.*

She sighed. *Why can't he ever be just nice? Why does*

he have to coat the nice thing he does in some jeering com-ment? Well, who cared anyway? The important thing was that it was done. She was grateful even if he did want to jeer at her. But then she looked at what they owed with late penalties and she wanted to cry again. If things kept going like this they would be in big trouble. Could they sell the farm and live off that? The farm that was beginning to feel like home to them? The farm that was almost becoming a member of the family? The *peaceful* member, she thought wryly. Sell it and live where? In some cramped apartment in town? Did St. Mary's By the Sea even *have* apartments? She'd never seen any. Where did Miss Webster live if not in an apartment? Then she remembered that Miss Webster and Mr. Pettinger would probably soon be adopting them before anything reached a crisis and she calmed down again. She would *give* Miss Webster and Mr. Pettinger the farm if they would just take this incessant worry away.

With the taxes done, there was a slight respite from things hanging over Fiona's head until one day another email came from Mr. Pennypacker. The subject was CITI-ZENSHIP. Fiona decided not to read this one either. Miss Webster was sure to make her announcement soon. And if Miss Webster adopted them then she and Mr. Pettinger could have all these bureaucratic worries. Fiona would just point them in the direction of Mr. Pennypacker and let them deal with it all. She could wait.

But her mind would go fretfully on its own sometimes to the subject line CITIZENSHIP. Would they be deported if she didn't deal with this? Was there more money involved? If the government found out they were living without an adult that was social services for sure. Best to steer clear of that one. Maybe Canada would just forget about them. They were just four small children in a large country. Perhaps no one really kept good track of these things.

When she began to spin in circles over this she trained her mind to start thinking of Davy instead. More and more she wondered if he felt about her the way she did about him or if he thought of her as just another friend, a new one from somewhere interesting, Borneo. Maybe he was more interested in Borneo than in her. He never put his arm around her, never took her hand, never tried to kiss her. She supposed since they only met at lunch and he probably did not want to be teased, particularly if she rebuffed him, he didn't dare try these things publicly but she worried nonetheless that he thought of her as a like-minded soul, not a girl per se. He had said that he didn't tell the sister in Natasha's class that he knew her because he didn't want his family to know because they might tease him about having a girlfriend. Did he mean by this that he didn't think of her as his girlfriend? Or that he did? She didn't know how to interpret this and was too embarrassed to ask.

Then one lunch while she was in the middle of a story about her teacher he interrupted her midsentence as if he hadn't been listening to a word she'd been saying and said, "There's a dance toward the end of June."

"I know," she said in surprise. "The Summer Fling. There's posters all over the school."

"It's mostly the older grades who go to it but anyone can. Do you want to go with me?"

Fiona was so surprised she just sat silently. Then her mind raced. Could she? Could she leave Marlin with Charlie and Natasha at night?

"Yes," she said before she'd even decided the baby-sitting issue. Yes, just because she wanted to. Yes, yes, work out everything else later, yes.

She realized as she watched his face that while she worried about logistics, he had been frightened she would say no to this invitation too.

He smiled.

"Okay," he said. "It's not until the Saturday after the last day of school. But I wanted to know."

She wondered if he would have asked someone else if she said no but then she thought, no. He didn't want to take just any girl to a dance. He wanted to take *her*. She tried not to look too pleased. She didn't want to frighten him by being too enthusiastic.

"Okay," she repeated.

Then the bell rang and they went back to class.

The Summer Fling sang in her head for the next week. So much so that she almost forgot that Marlin's birthday was on the horizon. When she remembered, she mentioned it one night at dinner. "Marlin, you've got a birthday coming."

"I know, don't worry," said Marlin, "we can't afford it."

"Marlin," said Fiona, shocked. "We can always afford birthdays. We can have *some* kind of a party. I mean we can have a *cake*. Your birthday's on Sunday, so Miss Webster and Mr. Pettinger could come too."

They all cheered up at the thought of a party. Fiona got together with Natasha and Charlie and they made birthday banners and presents for Marlin. Natasha made her a book of birds she might find in her own backyard. She drew pictures and wrote down what she'd observed about them. Fiona helped her with the writing. Charlie drew a picture of their family and another of Mrs. Weatherspoon for some reason. And they found some old frames in the attic for them. Fiona, who noticed that Marlin was out of hair elastics for her long hair, which she liked to keep in a ponytail, bought some at the grocery store and wrapped them in Aunt Martha's printer paper, which Charlie crayoned on to make wrapping paper. All in all it looked to be a splendid party. At least Fiona hoped Marlin would find it festive enough. Their family had never had a lot of money and parties had never been very elaborate but at least there used to be a small pile of presents for the birthday girl.

In the meantime, she had other worries. Fiona, unable to contain herself, had admitted to just one girl, Sarah, the one she thought she could trust with a secret, that she was going to the dance with Davy.

Sarah said, "Oh, fun. We figured you were an item 'cause you never eat lunch with us anymore. Are you buying a dress special? Most girls go into Shoreline with their moms. There's nowhere to get a dress in St. Mary's By the Sea."

Fiona hadn't given this part any thought at all.

"I don't know," she said.

"I mean, you don't have to buy a dress special," said Sarah. "You can wear an old one. It's just…" She paused delicately. There were few children at the school whose families had much money and what people could afford was always treated delicately. "People usually do," she finished reluctantly. "But it's not super dressy. Not like a prom. Not long dresses. But you know, nicer-than-ordinary dresses, more like party dresses."

Fiona nodded. She didn't know what to do about this. Did she dare to buy a dress? Even if she could get someone to take her into Shoreline she knew couldn't allow herself to spend the money. She couldn't tell Natasha and Charlie and Marlin they couldn't afford the things they wanted and then buy herself a dress.

"Well," she said with a sudden brainstorm. "Actually, I was thinking of more of an Audrey Hepburn retro-type look, you know, black pixie pants, flat shoes, fancy little top of some kind. Maybe a vest of some kind. Something maybe a little more *chic* than a dress."

"Oh," said Sarah, nodding but looking confused. "Right."

Now she hoped Sarah *would* tell people she was going to the dance. That she was going and wearing pants. She wanted people to know ahead of time. To think it was a carefully thought-out look and not that she simply couldn't afford to buy a dress. She wanted to go into the dance proudly, not feeling ashamed and not making Davy feel he had chosen to go with someone who couldn't even figure out how to dress properly for her first dance.

Every day she would ask Sarah, "Did you tell anyone I was going to the dance?" and Sarah would always say, "Oh, no. You asked me not to. Don't worry." So one day Fiona had to bring it up herself. Several girls were standing by the school's front door in the morning waiting to go in and one of the girls said, "Clayton finally asked me to the dance and my mother said we can go to Shoreline this weekend to dress-shop. Before all the good ones are gone."

"Well, I'm going to the dance too," said Fiona carefully. "Only I'm wearing pants. When my family lived in London, that was considered the thing to wear to dances. You know. Because why should only the boys be comfortable?"

There was a pause as the girls took in this astounding information and then one said, "But I like dresses. I always used to think about the kind of dress I would get for the Summer Fling when I was at Greenwillow."

"There's nothing wrong with dresses," said Fiona. "I just prefer pants. You know, nice pants."

"Wow," said another girl. "I guess I never thought about it."

"The Bloom Boutique in Shoreline gets in dresses every May for the June Summer Fling," said another girl. "I don't think they get in any pants."

"Well," said Fiona musingly. "Maybe they should."

"Wow," said the girl again. "Right."

Then they all went inside. *Mission accomplished,* thought Fiona. *And, after all,* she reminded herself as she rode home on the school bus that day looking at the trees and bushes laden and heavy with blossoms, *don't throw the baby out with the bathwater* as her father used to say. Lots of good things were happening. It was beautiful end-of-spring weather. Miss Webster would make her announcement soon—the one that would save them. They were all together—social services hadn't gotten them yet—and Davy had invited her to the dance. So what if she had to wear pants? She had gotten talk started and she bet by the time the dance came around she wouldn't be the only one wearing pants and if she was, the talk about her pants would hopefully be that she was merely following the chicest new trend from London. That those in the know wore pants. It was both a fashion-forward and a feminist statement. She was covered. She should just get on with planning Marlin's party.

As it turned out Miss Webster had her own idea about that when she and Mr. Pettinger came on Sunday and Marlin invited them to the party.

"It's not a big party, you know, with balloons," Fiona explained. "More of a quiet family affair." She had heard her mother use this expression many times.

"You don't have to bring presents," chimed in Charlie even though Fiona had told her not to say this.

"When you say to people 'don't bring presents' it always sounds like you expect them to," Fiona had told her.

"What if they want to bring presents?" Natasha had asked.

"You just don't say anything about presents," said Fiona.

"And hope maybe then they'll bring them," agreed Charlie knowingly.

"No, Charlie, you don't think about them one way or the other. It's about having your friends with you to celebrate. Not what you *get*," said Fiona but privately thinking

Charlie had it about right. Sometimes she got weary of being the keeper of the moral code.

But now, as usual, Charlie had forgotten.

"Well, you must let us bring the cake," said Miss Webster. "You can't make your own birthday cake, Marlin."

"Yes, I can," said Marlin excitedly. "I want to. I have this really fancy cake I want to try out and tweak. It's got seven thin layers and they're all different colors. It's called a rainbow cake. Only I want to make each layer also a different flavor. The only problem is Martha only has two kinds of extract in her cupboard. Vanilla and almond. I'm thinking maybe I can strain fruit and make some kind of extract on my own but it could be a mess. And I have no food coloring but—"

"I know!" interrupted Miss Webster excitedly. "Here's what we'll do. If you won't let me and Mr. Pettinger bring the cake, how about next Saturday, the day before your party, I take all four of you into Shoreline and instead of buying a cake, I'll buy you everything you need to make the one you want. We'll get extracts and food coloring and cake-decorating tools. The whole shebang! And we'll make a day of it. Mr. Pettinger works Saturday but we can have a girls' day out!"

"And I'll bring Chinese takeout for the party as my contribution," said Mr. Pettinger.

Marlin was so excited she clapped her hands.

"Can we have balloons?" cried Charlie.

"Charlie," said Fiona because Charlie knew they were never to ask for things.

"Yes, Charlie, we can have balloons," said Miss Webster, laughing.

"The expensive kind?" asked Charlie.

"Well, I don't know, Charlie," said Miss Webster, smiling at Mr. Pettinger over Charlie's head. "What's the expensive kind?"

"She means Mylar helium balloons," said Fiona defeatedly.

"We were never allowed the expensive kind," said Charlie.

"Oh, Charlie," said Fiona, sighing.

"Yes, we'll get a big bunch of those too," said Miss Webster, putting a reassuring hand on Fiona's leg to let her know it was all right.

"This is very nice of you," said Fiona. "But you really don't have to. Especially the balloons."

"I'm looking forward to it as much as the rest of you," said Miss Webster happily. "I haven't had a shopping spree in ages or the kind of party with balloons and it's the perfect way to celebrate because..." She stopped, looking at Mr. Pettinger as if to ask permission, and when he nodded she said, "We'll make our big announcement at the party too!"

Fiona immediately threw Charlie a warning look but Charlie said simply, "We've got a secret too!"

"Me too!" said Marlin happily. "And I'll make my big announcement too! Cake-decorating tools is the perfect gift. It's just what I need for my project."

"This is the moneymaking project?" asked Fiona. "Is this what your announcement is about?"

"I won't say another thing!" said Marlin smugly, miming locking her lips and throwing away the key.

That's it, thought Fiona. *She wants to start a cake-making business. Well, that's not so bad. It won't be the moneymaker she thinks but even if it brings her pocket money and makes her happy, it's a good thing. And I'll pretend when she announces it that I had no idea.*

<hr/>

The girls could hardly wait for the following Saturday to roll around. Miss Webster came for them in her car at nine o'clock and for the first time since they arrived at the airport they went through one side of St. Mary's By the Sea and out the other, taking the hourlong journey up-island to Shoreline. Because Marlin was the birthday girl she sat in front with Miss Webster. The others sat semi-squished in the back seat of Miss Webster's tiny car, peering out at everything as if for the first time.

"We were so jet-lagged when we arrived I don't remember any of the scenery," said Fiona.

"Look at the sandstone cliffs," said Natasha. "Pigeon guillemot nest there."

It seemed odd as they approached Shoreline to suddenly be in traffic after not seeing real traffic for months. There were large grocery stores and gas stations, cars whizzing this way and that.

Miss Webster turned into a strip mall and parked. "Look, Marlin. Shoreline has a whole store dedicated to cake decorating."

MISS MAISIE'S CAKES it said on a sign over the store.

Marlin couldn't contain her glee, leaping out and running to the door before the others could pile out.

Miss Webster laughed and said, "Well, I guess that was a success."

As Marlin went up and down the aisles, the others browsed all the cakes and cake posters on display.

"We have cake-decorating classes every Thursday," said a woman in an apron printed with cupcakes.

"Are you Miss Maisie?" asked Charlie.

"I am!" said the woman, laughing. "Are you a cake decorator?"

"Not me, my sister," said Charlie, pointing to Marlin, who was picking up and putting down bottles and reading labels.

Fiona found a chance to sidle over to Marlin and whisper, "Don't forget, Miss Webster is paying for this so don't get greedy."

"What do you take me for?" growled Marlin.

"I don't want to put a damper on your birthday," said Fiona. "But Mom would say that if she were here. You know she would."

"Don't worry," whispered Marlin. "You're not the only one brought up with manners."

"I know," said Fiona, and went off to pretend to be interested in the sprinkles section and then really became interested as Miss Maisie had fifty kinds.

"Okay," Marlin said finally when she'd perused everything. "I want this. It's the really good kind of food coloring I was reading about. You put a tiny dab into the icing with a toothpick and get good saturation."

"Just this?" said Miss Webster. "Oh, Marlin, you don't know how to have a birthday!" And Miss Webster got a basket and said, "Here, fill it. Get the things you think we can't find at Walmart. You can probably get extracts there, and some cake-decorating things, but the fancy stuff we should get here."

So Marlin, shrugging at Fiona as if to say, well, I tried, put in not everything she wanted, but enough things that it seemed a reasonable haul, and Miss Webster took it to the front and paid for it.

"Onward!" said Miss Webster.

At Walmart Miss Webster not only bought more cake-decorating tools and a cupcake tree, cupcake papers in many colors, sprinkles of all sorts, and a special wheel that you put a cake on so you could turn it to ice it, she also insisted on buying the girls new sneakers.

"We can't let you do this," said Fiona as Miss Webster helped Charlie find the right size.

"You can," said Miss Webster. "And you will. First of all, when I was in your position, I survived only because I had a lot of help and I promised someday to pay it forward so that's what today is. Payday. And I have another reason for wanting to do this today which you'll find out tomorrow," she added enigmatically.

Because they're adopting us, thought Fiona, and so decided to let go and just enjoy Miss Webster's beneficence.

"And now," said Miss Webster, "Mr. Pettinger wanted to do his part too so you must each pick either an item of clothing or a toy as his treat."

"But it's Marlin's birthday, not ours," protested Natasha.

"Yes, but these are *party favors,*" said Miss Webster. "You can't have a party without party favors."

Charlie chose the fashion doll she had been wanting for some time. Ashley had the exact same one and it came with both a red and a black ball gown. Natasha picked a pair of binoculars that were small enough to fit in her pocket but still powerful enough to see birds up close from far away. The ones she'd been using had belonged to Martha and were large and heavy and clunky and hard to cart around. While Marlin was choosing a new summer shirt, Fiona wandered away from the others and sneaked to the area of dresses but there was nothing nice enough for the dance or cheap enough to let Mr. Pettinger pay for so she quickly abandoned that idea and picked out a new shirt from the same rack Marlin had chosen from. Then Miss Webster finished the shopping spree by buying them all rain boots, something they sorely needed and none of them had. They loaded all the purchases into the car and went to a drive-through burger restaurant for lunch, finishing at a dollar store, where Miss Webster got a large bouquet of Mylar helium balloons.

"This has been the happiest day of my life," said Charlie expansively on the way home, sitting in the middle of the balloon bouquet.

"Oh, Charlie," said Fiona, laughing, but she felt a tug at the idea of any of their days since their parents died being the happiest.

"Well, it's certainly been one of the most gratifying ones I've ever had," said Miss Webster, laughing too. "And will make a wonderful memory."

Then they pulled up at the McCready farm and all got out of the car. Miss Webster helped carry things into the house and prepared to leave, saying, "Don't forget, Mr. Pettinger and I are bringing Chinese food for dinner so all you need to supply is the cake."

Marlin, who had taken her supplies out of the bags and boxes, was busy washing the decorating tools and preheating the oven.

"Oh boy," she said. "I've wanted to try this cake for the longest time. I'm only sorry I didn't get to try it in time for my project…" And then she stopped herself.

"Is that a clue about your big announcement?" asked Miss Webster.

"Never mind," said Marlin. "I didn't mean to say that. Some secret keeper I am."

"Well, I understand," said Miss Webster. "I didn't mean to say that about the day making a good memory either. I almost gave myself away too!"

And then she was off.

Fiona and Natasha sat on the front steps watching Miss Webster drive away. Charlie had run upstairs to take her doll out of the box and play with it.

Fiona was puzzled. "What did Miss Webster mean by it making a wonderful memory? That was an odd thing to say."

"I don't know. Maybe she means we're building family memories, you know, if they adopt us, which would, anyhow, feel weird," said Natasha, looking suddenly solemn. "I mean I like them both, Miss Webster and Mr. Pettinger. Don't get me wrong. But…they're not going to be like replacing Mom and Dad, right? I mean, they aren't really family. I don't *want* them to be family. Not in that way. It doesn't feel right. It feels too make-believe or something."

"No, I know what you mean," said Fiona swiftly. "But Nat, we've got to have an adult legally. It's important."

"Why can't we just go on as we are?"

"You know that would be fine with me but there's things, business things I would find easier if I had a grown-up in charge."

"Maybe you should show the business things to me. Maybe I could help," said Natasha.

"No, trust me, if I can't figure some things out, you haven't a chance."

"And where are we going to put Miss Webster and Mr. Pettinger if they move in?" asked Natasha. "Nobody's figured that out yet. I mean even if Mr. Pettinger can build another bedroom where do they sleep in the meantime?"

"I don't know, Nat. I guess we'll have to worry about that later. I don't know what to tell you except that having them here is the lesser of two evils." Fiona felt ungrateful putting it that way after all Miss Webster had done for them and especially on a day when she'd bought them so much stuff. But she knew what Natasha meant. Miss Webster and Mr. Pettinger, while wonderful people and their first choice for guardians, were still not family. It would still be awkward and weird living with them. Like having permanent house guests.

"I'm going to go look for birds with my new binoculars," said Natasha, and jumped off the porch, leaving Fiona alone.

I'm not going to worry for the rest of the day, thought Fiona. *Worry can get to be a habit like anything else if that's all you do. I'm not doing any more today. I'm taking a holiday.* And she too went to put away her new sneakers and purple rain boots and pink summer shirt and to make sure the balloon bouquet was securely tied to a kitchen chair. This had been a wonderful day and tomorrow with the party would be an even better one.

The Party

SUNDAY dawned as beautiful a June day as you could find. Charlie was restlessly running around the house, always with her fashion doll in hand, more excited than anyone about the party. Fiona and Natasha were doing their usual Sunday clean of the house and Marlin was putting cake layers together and decorating the top and sides of the cake with her new cake-decorating tools.

"Charlie, can you set the table?" said Fiona as she and Natasha strung the banners.

Charlie ran in and she and her new doll began putting down knives and forks, the knives to the right of the plate and the forks to the left just as she'd been taught.

"That's seven place settings, Charlie, we only need six," said Fiona.

Charlie counted on her fingers and then said, "No, seven."

"The four of us and Miss Webster and Mr. Pettinger," said Fiona. "Four plus two is six."

"And Al," said Charlie.

"Al's not coming," said Fiona.

"Yes, he is, I invited him," said Charlie.

"YOU INVITED AL to MY party?" roared Marlin in dismay.

"Yes. I saw him when I took the garbage down. I thought he was already invited so I was talking about the party and then he didn't know about it so I said he should come."

"What did he say?" asked Fiona.

"He said he'd think about it," said Charlie.

"Oh, there, you see, you don't have to worry, Marlin," said Fiona, sighing. "You know he won't come."

"No, I guess not," said Marlin, and went back to carefully crafting rosebuds on the cake.

"But you shouldn't go inviting people without asking us," Fiona admonished Charlie.

"Well, I didn't know you didn't want him. You said you were glad he did the taxes. And he's my friend. I thought you'd want him here."

"Never mind," said Fiona. "Set seven places. We can remove one if he doesn't come." She gave Marlin a significant look, which was wasted on her, so caught up was she in cake details.

After that the wrapped presents were piled in the center of the table.

"What's this one?" Fiona whispered to Charlie, noting the extra parcel.

"I drew a picture of Billy Bear and put it in another attic frame," said Charlie. "It's for Al. It's his party favor."

"We don't have party favors for Miss Webster and Mr. Pettinger," said Natasha.

So Charlie ran off to draw pictures and find frames for them too. She drew a picture of Miss Webster for Mr. Pettinger and one of Mr. Pettinger for Miss Webster.

"That's nice," said Fiona distractedly as she arranged a bouquet of wildflowers for the table and Charlie added the party favors at Miss Webster's and Mr. Pettinger's places.

At five o'clock Mr. Pettinger and Miss Webster arrived. Instead of spending all Sunday afternoon with the girls, they were coming later than usual because they wanted to pick up the Chinese food at the last minute so it would arrive hot. It was to be an early dinner.

It was a happy party. Miss Webster seemed particularly joyful, hugging each of the girls in turn. Marlin caught Fiona's eye and her expression said, see? Adoption coming. Fiona ignored her, worried they would give it away or encourage Charlie to burst out with the news before Miss Webster could announce it.

Fiona and Natasha put plates down while Marlin sat at her place of honor at the head of the table and Mr. Pettinger and Miss Webster opened carton after carton of Chinese food from a seemingly endless supply and stuck serving spoons in them.

"We didn't know what you'd like," explained Mr. Pettinger.

"So we just got an assortment of dishes," said Miss Webster.

"Like just about everything on the menu it looks," said Marlin.

"It's a special day!" said Miss Webster. "A special, special day!"

"Where's Al?" asked Charlie. "I think he forgot. I think I should go next door and get him."

"Is Al Farber coming?" asked Miss Webster in surprise.

"He said he *might* come," said Fiona. "Don't go get him, Charlie. I'm sure he didn't forget. If he's not here he must have a reason."

"Yes, don't go get him," said Marlin.

"But he'll miss dinner!" protested Charlie.

"Hey, birthday girl rules!" said Marlin, and that quieted Charlie because the family birthday rule was that the birthday girl got to choose all the particulars of the party and events of the day within reason. This sometimes made for some strange birthdays. There were three years in a row when Natasha not only said no vegetables for dinner but didn't even allow the others to eat them. There were to be no vegetables VISIBLE ANYWHERE. And there was the year in Fiji when Marlin made them all wear coconut-shell party hats she had tried somewhat unsuccessfully to make. They were still rather damp when they arrived at the table. Their mother said never mind, coconut milk was supposed to be very good for the hair.

So dinner began without Al although Charlie insisted on leaving his place setting just in case. Cartons were passed and the girls marveled as they ate ginger beef, egg rolls, sweet-and-sour pork, chicken fried rice, egg foo young, wonton soup, kung pao chicken, almond chicken, prawns with snow peas, mushroom chop suey, and shrimp chow mein. They all had their plates heaped high and Miss Webster offered to teach them how to use chopsticks but of course they already knew because of all the places they had lived around the world. When everyone was done, they pushed their chairs back and Charlie said sadly, "There's still so much food left."

Everyone laughed.

"We're leaving the leftovers with you. You can have them tomorrow," said Mr. Pettinger.

"We can have them all week it looks like," said Fiona, gazing at the many half-full cartons.

"Good," said Miss Webster. "Marlin won't have to cook for a change. Now, cake, anyone?"

"Let's take a break," said Marlin. "I couldn't eat another bite right now."

"Well, time for announcements then?" asked Miss

Webster. "We have two and I know the birthday girl has one. So, who's first?"

"YOU! YOU!" cried Charlie.

Fiona threw her a warning look.

"All right," began Miss Webster when there was a loud knock on the door.

Who in the world, thought Fiona, and then groaned inwardly. Of course. They hadn't told Al what time dinner was and he probably thought it was at six. Well, this was embarrassing. Although there was certainly enough food for him it still seemed so rude that they had eaten without him. She hadn't for one minute believed he would really come.

"It's Al!" said Charlie, happily leaping up and running to the front door.

Al, who was dressed in his usual dirty T-shirt and ragged pants, came in and stood a second in the doorway looking at the table and the remains of food sitting on people's plates.

"Oh!" he said.

"Come in," said Fiona graciously. "We didn't think you were coming but there's lots of food left."

"Didn't know, uh, time," said Al, stumbling slightly as he came into the room.

Miss Webster frowned. She looked at Mr. Pettinger.

He rose and in the guise of shaking Al's hand, steadied him, brought him to his chair, and passed him chopsticks and some cartons. Al shrugged, filled his plate, and began eating voraciously.

"You make this?" he asked Marlin.

"It's in Chinese *takeout* cartons!" said Marlin in disgust.

"We were just having announcements," said Miss Webster before Marlin could say something ruder.

"Yeah, okay, don't mind me," said Al, shoveling food in.

Charlie moved her chair next to Al's and put his party favor in front of him.

"What's this?" he asked with chow mein noodles hanging out of his mouth.

"It's a picture I made for you of Billy Bear," she said.

He opened it and looked at it in astonishment. "Wow, that's..." He sat looking at it as if he didn't know quite what to say.

"Announcements?" interrupted Marlin.

"It looks just like Billy," said Charlie happily, bouncing in her chair.

"Exactly," agreed Al, and went back to shoveling food into his mouth.

"Ahem," said Miss Webster, hitting the side of her water glass with her knife to make a chiming sound. "Okay, well, Mr. Pettinger and I have two big, big announcements. First of all, you can finally call us Diana and Don."

"Because you're *FAMILY*!" squealed Charlie.

"I hope you will always think of us as family, Charlie, yes," said Miss Webster, not understanding Charlie's implication. "Our announcement, as I say, has two parts. The first part is that Don and I are getting married!"

"I knew it. I knew it. But Fiona said that couldn't be it because *you've only just met!*" said Charlie, bouncing up and down in her chair.

Miss Webster burst into laughter. "You've been in charge too long, Fiona," she said. "You're turning into a mother."

Fiona blushed. "She means congratulations," she said, throwing Charlie a look.

"Thank you."

"I guess you're going to have your big happy ending," said Fiona, trying to remember the type of thing her mother would say on such an occasion and remembering Mrs. Weatherspoon had said this when she thought they'd landed safely with Martha.

"Well, I don't think of it as an end—more as a beginning, and anyhow, I don't believe in one big happy ending." Miss Webster smiled at Mr. Pettinger. "I'll settle for a lot of little happy middles."

"A lot of little happy middles," repeated Fiona dazedly. This was it, the second part of the announcement, what they had been waiting for was coming. A lot of little happy middles? One for each McCready?

"Can we be the flower girls?" asked Charlie, who had always wanted to be one.

"Well, unfortunately, no, because—and that takes me to part two of the announcement."

"You're buying ponies!" said Charlie before she could stop herself. "No, wait, that would be part three."

"*HUSH*, Charlie," said Fiona ferociously, "and let Miss Webster finish!" For now a sinking feeling was coming over her. She did not see how not being flower girls could lead to an announcement of Mr. Pettinger and Miss Webster adopting the McCreadys.

"Part two is that Don and I are moving up to the Yukon. Don was offered a job there, back close to where he used to live. It's a wonderful opportunity and he has been wanting to return home and I have always wanted to see the Yukon. Now I will be living there!"

There were no glad cries now. There was a long silence instead. Charlie just looked confused.

"But are we *all* going?" she asked finally.

"What?" asked Miss Webster. "Oh, Charlie, no. We're getting married up there, which is why you can't be flower girls. If we were to marry *here* of course you would be. But you see I have no family and Don's family is all in the Yukon so it only makes sense to marry there. I will send you lots of photos, I promise," she ended lamely.

There was another uncomfortable silence, which Miss

Webster tried to fill with cheerful enthusiastic natter, but it rang hollow in the room and fooled no one. "And I'm so proud of all of you. I can see you're doing fine now. Of course, I can't check on you every week as I have been but we can keep in touch with emails and I will phone you every Sunday. Finding my replacement as principal of Greenwillow has been the difficulty and I didn't want to announce any of this until one could be found but the school board thinks Mrs. Edwards will be a wonderful fit for the school and she can start next week. I've got Al named in the file as your guardian and I don't think Mrs. Edwards, who will have so many other things on her mind, being new to the school and new to the community, will question it or even notice it but if she does I will vouch for him. I hate leaving the four of you but this is an opportunity we can't pass up and I hope you will be happy for us."

"Of course we are," said Fiona automatically.

But looking at the table it was hard to see any happiness. Al was still shoveling in food unaffected. Charlie still looked confused. Natasha was back in one of her little worlds as if she hadn't heard a word and Marlin looked dumbstruck.

Finally Fiona, hoping to save the situation, said, "Well, that is such wonderful news and now, Marlin, time for *your* happy announcement!"

Marlin visibly pulled herself together and stood up as if just suddenly remembering her own happy news.

"Well!" she said. "I have spent the last couple of months writing a cookbook. It's called *Thirty Meals a Twelve-Year-Old Could Make and* Did! I'm particularly proud of the title. And I sent it to a publisher and it's going to be published and I'll make a ton of money because I can think of lots of other cookbooks to write. And other kinds of books. Like maybe a series, like *Thirty Things a Twelve-Year-Old Could Fix and* Has! It's all to show that people twelve years old can do all this stuff that we've had to learn. Of course, that's the hook. But the cooking and baking is the part I'm really interested in. Still, it should be a moneymaker, this series, and I can support us and Nat can go to strings."

"You're getting a book published!" said Miss Webster in amazement. "That's *wonderful!*"

"What publisher?" asked Al through a mouthful of food.

"Random House," said Marlin.

"Random House sent you a contract?" asked Al, looking startled.

"I haven't actually heard from them yet but I sent the manuscript there," said Marlin proudly. "I couldn't decide for a while which publisher to choose but I like the cookbooks they've published so I decided to give it to them."

Al snorted. "You know how many manuscripts they get sent? It won't even get *read*, Marlin. You need an agent just to get *read* and even then, the likelihood of getting published is practically nil."

"It is *NOT!*" said Marlin, bristling angrily and standing up. "You don't know anything. You only had one book published and that was ten years ago. And what's the matter with you? Did you just come to *RUIN MY BIRTHDAY*?"

"Yes, maybe another time, Mr. Farber," said Miss Webster gently.

"Ha, another time?" said Al through a mouthful of chow mein. "Talk about timing. You just told the kid on her birthday that you'll be abandoning her and her sisters. So don't talk to me about timing."

Miss Webster looked suddenly shocked and horrified. "They know we're not abandoning them!" she said.

"Oh, they do, do they? You're moving way up to the Yukon, aren't you? Don't think I don't know what's been going on here. Charlie tells me everything. She thought you were adopting them. She thought that's what you were going to announce today."

"Oh no," whispered Miss Webster. "Charlie, did you really think that?"

Charlie began to cry.

"There, you see," said Al, pointing his chopstick at her. "Happy birthday, indeed."

"Oh, Charlie," said Miss Webster, going over to hug her.

Fiona glanced at Marlin, who still looked furious, and wondered frantically how to save the disintegrating party. The party they'd all been looking forward to all week.

"How about some cake?" she said with fake cheer.

"No, thanks," said Al, pushing his chair back and putting down his chopsticks. "I'm going home. I'm clearly persona non grata."

He grabbed his framed picture of Billy Bear and rose. Then, as if he'd almost forgotten, he reached into his back pocket and pulled out a ring box, tossing it on the table. "Here, kid, this is for you. Happy birthday. I bought it for Martha but she didn't want it so I figured it should go to one of you. You can sell it if you want. I paid two thousand dollars for it. Don't take less than fifteen hundred if you sell it."

And he stomped out of the house.

Mr. Pettinger passed the box to Marlin, who opened it. Inside was a diamond ring.

"It must be the ring he asked Aunt Martha to marry him with," said Marlin, examining it in awe.

"It's a highly inappropriate gift for a thirteen-year-old. Don't wear it to school, Marlin," said Miss Webster.

"I wouldn't wear it anywhere. I don't even like jewelry," said Marlin.

"But, as he says, you can sell it…" said Miss Webster. "It *was* a generous gift…"

"We may as well open the rest of the presents if you want, Marl," said Fiona.

"Sure," said Marlin. "I mean it's still my birthday. He didn't ruin it even if he tried." Then she ruffled all over again. "He doesn't know I won't get published! He thinks he's such a know-it-all just because he wrote for the *New York Times*. But he doesn't know how good my book is. He doesn't know anything about it."

"Of course he doesn't," said Fiona. "There are always naysayers about any project."

"That was a rotten thing to say on my birthday," said Marlin.

"Well, you didn't have to be mean to him," said Charlie. "He gave you a ring! Mom always said to be polite to guests."

"He wasn't polite to me," said Marlin. "You're supposed to be polite as a guest too. And I'm the birthday girl. I'm not keeping the ring. The next time I bring him dinner I'm returning the ring to him."

"Let's clear the table and put out cake plates," said Miss Webster swiftly. "I'm dying to try this cake you keep talking about!"

It was obvious to Fiona that Marlin was less upset now about Miss Webster and Mr. Pettinger moving away than she was about having her book-publishing bubble popped. And she had the feeling that Charlie still wasn't sure what was going on. That despite Miss Webster's explanation, in Charlie's head they were all going to the Yukon together.

It had been a table of woeful faces but everyone perked up when the cake was brought out.

"Hold on," said Marlin, getting the cell phone. She took a photo. "I've been taking pictures of all my food. I'm probably going to do a cake book next. *Thirty Cakes a Twelve-Year-Old Could Bake and* Did!"

"You're thirteen," pointed out Natasha.

"Yes, but I was twelve when I baked it. Besides, twelve sounds better in the title. Thirteen sounds like you're no longer a kid. You have to think about these things when you start writing books," said Marlin importantly.

"I think your book ideas are wonderful," said Miss Webster. "And your titles are very catchy."

"And the cake is amazing," said Mr. Pettinger. "It looks professional. Doesn't it look professional, Diana?"

"It does!" agreed Miss Webster.

"Thanks," said Marlin, looking mollified.

Fiona put the thirteen candles on the cake and lit them. Marlin blew them out and then said, "I bet we can all guess what I wished for!"

"You're not supposed to tell," said Charlie.

"I'm not telling, Charlie," said Marlin. "I'm saying we can all guess. Okay, I hate to ruin the presentation but time to slice the cake. Actually, that's the best part. That's when you see the magic."

The cake was, as Marlin promised, magic—a wonder of layers. Marlin took a long careful time slicing pieces. She began by slicing two pieces before removing the first one, the way she had read to slice a cake if you don't want the pieces to fall apart when you remove them. Then she handed round beautiful rainbow slices, each slice with seven layers and each layer a different color and flavor. For a moment they all looked at the cake slices in front of them, unwilling to mar their perfection with a bite.

"They're beautiful," said Fiona.

"Vanilla, chocolate, coconut, cherry, lemon, almond, and orange," said Marlin. "I put a plain vanilla butter-cream between the layers because I didn't want the icing to clash with the cake flavors."

"Which color is which flavor?" asked Natasha.

"Take a bite and guess," said Marlin, digging in.

By the time they were done guessing and had discovered that white was vanilla, brown was chocolate, green was coconut, red was cherry, yellow was lemon, blue was almond, and orange was orange, they were all feeling a little better.

Marlin opened her presents from her sisters and happily

exclaimed over them. Miss Webster and Mr. Pettinger opened the pictures Charlie had made and declared them amazing likenesses. Then, finally, it was time for Miss Webster and Mr. Pettinger to go.

At the door Miss Webster pulled Fiona aside. "You do know I'm not abandoning you, right?"

Fiona nodded but her heart sank again. All the worries she had thought would soon be off her shoulders were now securely back on. "When are you leaving?"

"Next Saturday. You really will be okay, Fiona, all of you. I wouldn't go if I weren't sure of it."

"I know," said Fiona. "Don't worry."

They hugged and then there were hugs all around and Miss Webster and Mr. Pettinger left. Fiona, Natasha, and Charlie hurried to wash and put away the dishes. Marlin, of course, was the birthday girl and so excused. Then Charlie and Natasha went to bed. Fiona could hear Charlie quizzing Natasha over and over about why Miss Webster and Mr. Pettinger weren't adopting them. Fiona was thankful that it was Natasha who shared a room with Charlie and not her. She didn't think she could stand a half hour reassuring someone when her own spirits were so low.

"Well, it wasn't the suckiest birthday I ever had," said Marlin once she and Fiona were lying exhaustedly under covers.

"I know," said Fiona.

"The worst one was the one right after Mommy and Dad died."

"Yep."

"Trying to pretend I was happy that Mrs. Weatherspoon made me three cakes."

"Yep. That was definitely worse than this," said Fiona.

"I really thought they would adopt us and move in, didn't you?"

"I told everyone not to assume," said Fiona wearily. She did not want to divulge even to Marlin how cruel her disappointment had been.

"I guess those presents they bought us were like good-bye presents, not welcome-to-the-family presents," said Marlin bitterly.

"Marlin, they had no obligation to do anything for us."

"I know, but jeez, they're still kind of just abandoning us like Al said."

"No, they aren't. They're getting on with their lives and we will too."

"I still think it kind of sucks on their part."

"It doesn't really. They didn't even know we were thinking about adoption."

"And what's with Al and his no one but he can be published? I'm not keeping his sucky ring either. I can't wait to throw it back at him. I will be the second McCready to do so. Maybe he ought to start wondering why no one likes him, maybe he should…"

"Marlin…we need the money. We're keeping the ring."

There was a silence, then Marlin said, "Okay." There was another silence before she added, "But it galls me to do so."

"I know," said Fiona. "I'm sorry. But it *was* still, as Miss Webster said, a generous present."

"I don't think I can ever call them Diana and Don."

"I don't think you'll have to worry about that much longer anyway," said Fiona.

And then they were both quiet and the stars moved on their slow nightly trip, the Big Dipper traversing from one corner of the window to the other until finally both girls, lost in their private tangle of thoughts, fell asleep.

The Dance

AT the end of the week there was an assembly at Green-willow Elementary. Natasha told Fiona about it on the bus ride home. The new principal was introduced and the school said good-bye to Miss Webster. On Saturday Miss Webster and Mr. Pettinger stopped by the farm briefly to say good-bye. Miss Webster left them her sewing machine, saying it was too heavy to pack, and Mr. Pettinger left them some tools he didn't want to take with him or sell. And then they were off to the airport.

"It seems so strange," said Marlin. "It's like they were this fixture and then poof, they're gone."

"A little too much of that going on," muttered Fiona before she remembered to be positive again.

Fiona was a bit worried that the new principal would, despite Miss Webster's assurances, somehow find out about them and call social services but when a week and a half passed and nothing happened she began to relax. The end of school was coming up that Friday and the dance was the Saturday night following and then they were free until

September. The younger girls were excited about summer vacation and Fiona was excited about the dance. More excited than she had been about anything for a long time.

On the last day of school as they got off the bus and headed down their driveway to the house, Fiona finally told her sisters.

"When did he ask you?" asked Natasha.

"A few weeks ago," said Fiona.

"Well!" said Marlin. "Thanks for telling *us*."

"I was going to," said Fiona. "I just hadn't gotten around to it yet."

"What are you going to wear?" asked Marlin.

"You know, my good clothes," said Fiona.

"I heard all the girls go dress-shopping in Shoreline," said Natasha.

"All but one," said Fiona cheerfully.

"You can't wear pants," said Marlin.

"Can and will," said Fiona.

Marlin looked at the ground, deep in thought, and then said, "I'm selling the ring. You can use some of the money from that. I mean you can get a dress now and we'll just say that the ring money covers it."

"No, I can't, Marlin. I guess I was hoping maybe I could get a dress at the last second if Miss Webster and Mr. Pettinger adopted us. That Miss Webster would find out I was going to the dance and suggest dress-shopping.

But we need to be realistic. They didn't. They're gone. There will be no dress. And we have to be careful with money and spend wisely only on the necessities and a dress I would wear once is not a necessity. Anyhow, it's not the end of the world. I told all the girls that everyone in London wore pants to dances. I'm going to be the chic new girl in pants. Even if we had the money for a dress we have no way to get to Shoreline to shop for it."

"Well…" Marlin thought about it. "Your good black pants are okay but that white shirt is kind of blah and the vest is out of style. I mean at the time you got it it was okay for *church* but you don't want to wear it to a dance. No one wears vests anymore."

"I already thought of that," said Fiona. "I'll just wear the white shirt but out, not tucked in."

"Maybe Martha had something we can redo instead with the sewing machine Miss Webster left us. I'm not good at sewing but you are," said Marlin. "You know, something sparkly or chiffon or more dressy somehow. From the look of the clothes we bagged in her bedroom, she was pretty tiny. Her stuff would fit you. Or maybe she's got a scarf or something you can dress it up with."

"I hate scarves," said Fiona. "They fidget me and I think they look old-lady-like anyhow. When we bagged Martha's clothes and moved them from her bedroom to the attic I didn't see anything I would want to wear anywhere let alone to a dance. There was nothing but ratty T-shirts and sweatshirts."

"What about the attic? There's a bunch of boxes there we haven't gone through. Maybe she had some old glamorous clothes she stored there that we could redo. She must have had *some* good clothes. She had two men after her, for Pete's sake. She couldn't have worn ratty T-shirts *all* the time."

"I didn't think of that," Fiona admitted.

Charlie and Natasha weren't interested in looking through the attic. Charlie went to play with her fashion doll and Natasha went out to the meadow with her binoculars, leaving the two older girls to spend the rest of Friday afternoon pawing through boxes of things, most of it dusty old books and dishes and rusty gardening tools.

"People put things in attics that they ought to just throw away if you ask me," said Marlin when they'd finished rummaging through the last of the boxes without finding any clothes at all.

"Well, that's that anyway," said Fiona. "It's my white shirt and black pants or nothing. Anyway, the important thing is that I'm going to the dance. You know what Mom said, don't throw the baby out with the bathwater. You don't mind staying alone with Charlie and Natasha at night, do you? You've never done it before."

"Pfff," snorted Marlin. "Kids babysit at thirteen all the

time. I'm going to the secondary school next year. I guess that means I'm old enough."

"I guess," said Fiona.

"I stay with them when you grocery-shop."

"This is at night."

"Stop being such a worrywart and speaking of night, how are you getting there? You're not biking down that dark road with the bears and cougars, are you?"

"Well, it will still be light when the dance starts," said Fiona.

"Yeah, but not when it's done."

"Yeah, I know. I hate to do it but I think I'm going to have to ask Al to drive me. He owes us still for the chocolate chip cookies."

"Waste troll," said Marlin.

"I know it's your turn to take him his dinner tonight but I think I'd better so I can ask him. I've been meaning to every time I took dinner over this week but I kept losing my nerve and this is my last night before the dance so I'd better just do it. I hate to ask him for anything, he gets so shouty."

"I'll ask him if you like. I'm not afraid of him."

"I'm not afraid of him, I just know it's going to be an ordeal."

All the way to Al's, Fiona practiced how she would ask him. "So, you know that favor you owe us?" Or, "Remember those chocolate chip cookies?" Or just straight up, "I need you to drive me to the school dance and pick me up tomorrow night."

She was still rehearsing ways to ask him when she knocked on his door so that when he opened it and shouted "WHAT!" she startled so badly she almost dropped his dinner.

"*Jeez Louise!*" she blurted out. "I wish you'd stop doing that."

"Doing what?"

"Shouting 'WHAT!' every time you open the door. We've been bringing you dinner for months."

"What is it tonight?" he said, peering into the food container. "Ah, Marlin's pork chops. My favorite."

"Speaking of favorites," said Fiona, which she realized made no sense but she couldn't think of another way to segue, "I was wondering if you could drive me to the school dance tomorrow night. And pick me up. It starts at seven and is over by ten."

"School dance, huh?"

"Yeah."

"Who's staying with the others if you're out dancing?"

"Marlin's thirteen now. She's old enough to babysit."

"Is she? Well, I wouldn't know these magical demarcations between twelve and thirteen. Anyhow, what did I tell you about chauffeur service?"

"You owe us for the chocolate chip cookies."

Al was quiet for a second, reconnoitering. "So I do," he said finally. "Well, never let it be said I don't pay my debts. Okay. I'll pick you up at what time?"

"Six-forty-five." And right then Fiona, because she was so relieved that he had said yes without fuss, rattled on without thinking. "I told Davy I'd meet him there at seven."

"Oho!" said Al. "You're going with a boy, are you?"

"Yes," said Fiona, blushing and hoping without much hope this would be the end of it.

"Old enough for that, are you?"

"Yes," said Fiona.

"Well, well, well. A little romance brewing, is there?"

"I don't really want to talk about it," she said.

"Nice boy?"

"Yes," she spat out, losing her control in exasperation.

"I see. Well, why isn't he coming to get you then? That's what a proper gentleman does. And comes to your door, doesn't just sit outside in the driveway honking either. Tell him that."

"He's not old enough to drive. He's only fifteen."

"Well, why doesn't one of his parents take you?"

"He isn't telling his family about us."

"Ashamed of you?"

She started to reply hotly when she saw he was teasing her.

"And besides, I can't let him come to the house for obvious reasons. I can't even tell him about our living situation."

"I see," said Al. "Kind of hard to lead a normal life with such a big secret going on, isn't it?"

"Maybe," said Fiona.

"Charlie's not the only one disappointed not to be adopted, I would guess."

"Whatever. By the way, Marlin said to tell you we're eating at four-thirty tomorrow and she's bringing your dinner early."

"Why?"

"I don't want to go to the dance on a full stomach," said Fiona.

Al laughed and then said, "Say, has Marlin sold that ring yet?"

"Not yet. But she's going to put it up on eBay. I think she forgot to thank you but we all really appreciate it. It was very generous of you."

"Nah, what was I going to do with it anyway? Any word from Random House?"

"Not yet," said Fiona.

"Shame to get her hopes up. Okay, well, tomorrow."

"Thanks," said Fiona, and turned her back to walk self-consciously away. She didn't hear Al's door close and she could feel his eyes on her back all the way down the driveway. Sometimes he could be not so bad, she thought. Almost normal really.

The next morning all the girls were as excited as if they were going to the dance too. All day long they fussed about Fiona, suggesting things she could do to appear more glamorous, but Fiona refused to tease her hair, pluck her eyebrows, or practice walking with a book on her head, the last an idea Charlie had gotten from a TV show. They had found some old bright red lipstick belonging to Martha and that evening Fiona tried it on but decided it looked silly on her. She did let Marlin rub a little into her cheeks.

"It's supposed to go on the cheekbones, so," said Marlin. "So that you get these model-like checkbones. Why do you suppose she had lipstick but no good clothes? Who wears bright red lipstick with ratty old T-shirts?"

Natasha had picked some wild roses and put them in Fiona's hair.

"Thanks, Nat. They look really pretty," said Fiona, who planned to take them out once she was out of sight of the house.

"You look good," said Charlie. "Even if they are just your old Sunday clothes."

"You smell nice," said Natasha. "That's the wild roses. Smelling nice is actually probably even more important than looking nice. It is in the animal world."

"You look very chic. Very London chic," said Marlin.

"I reminded Al he was driving when I took his dinner over at four-thirty. When's he supposed to come? It's ten to seven already."

"He's late," said Fiona glumly. "Knowing him, he forgot anyway. I guess I'll walk over there and remind him."

"Have fun. Have fun!" called the girls from the porch steps as Fiona made her way carefully down the driveway, trying to keep her good shoes nice.

I will, thought Fiona happily, *I'm just going to forget everything tonight and have fun.* She had already watched endless YouTube videos of people dancing. Slow dancing, fast dancing. Just to make sure she knew how it was done. Her stomach was flipping over with nerves now as she imagined her arms around Davy's neck and wondered whether at any point they would be alone and if he would kiss her. She had studied old movie clips on YouTube of people kissing to make sure she wouldn't do anything stupid if he did. Davy had bought the tickets to the dance and not let her pay him back, which she thought was very romantic. She wondered if Al would manage to keep his mouth shut when he dropped her off. She hoped so. Maybe she should ask him to drop her off a block away from the school. Yes, that's what she would do. Then she'd meet Al a block away afterward as well and there would be no chance he could tease her or embarrass her in front of Davy.

When she got to his driveway she saw Al's pickup

truck sitting where it always did. *At least I know he's still here,* she thought, and went up the trailer steps and knocked loudly on the door. There was no answer. She knocked again. When he didn't come out she went to the garage and peered in but he wasn't in there or in the truck. Finally, she went back to the trailer and opened the door a crack and peeked in and there he was lying on the couch snoring away.

Oh, for heaven's sake, she thought, *he* would *forget and take a nap.* She went over and tapped him on the shoulder. "Hello! Hello!" she said loudly. "It's time for the dance. We're late!"

Al opened his eyes a crack, rolled over, and went back to sleep.

She stood in confusion for a moment and then she saw the pile of empty beer cans next to the couch and smelled the aroma of beer like a little fog around him. *No, no,* she thought, *he's drunk. No, he can't be. Not tonight.*

She poked him hard this time but he didn't wake up and she began to cry. Even if he did wake up he couldn't drive her, drunk as he was. It was already seven o'clock. Davy was going to wonder where she was. He was going to stand there waiting and she wouldn't show up and he wouldn't know why. What would he think? How long would he wait in front of the school for her? Could she bike there and tell him what had happened? She started to sob consumed by injured merit, all the tension and the disappointment and the nagging fears of that year suddenly washing over her at this final unexpected disappointment.

"It's not *fair!*" she shouted in an incoherent tangle of frustration at the snoring Al. "I let Miss Webster go without complaining. I didn't mind worrying about money or doing the books or avoiding Mr. Pennypacker because I had this one thing to look *forward to!*"

She screamed the last two words so loudly it frightened her and caused Al to roll over and look at her confusedly through one partially opened eye.

"Fiona?" he murmured.

"You were supposed to drive me!" she yelled. "To the DANCE! I should have known you'd never come through for me. I knew I'd never get this." She was choking so hard on her sobs that she could hardly think straight or get her words out. "I tried so hard to do everything right this year. For Marlin and Nat and Charlie. I didn't even BUY A *DRESS!*" She turned midsob and fled.

━━━✦━━━

When Fiona got back home she ran up and locked herself into the bathroom, where she continued to sob brokenheartedly. The girls, who had followed behind her, knocked on the bathroom door.

"What happened?" called Marlin.

"What do you think?" yelled Fiona. "He was DRUNK. He was passed out."

"Oh, no. But what about Davy?" asked Marlin.

"I was going…" Fiona's sentences broke up as she gulped between sobs, "bike up…tell him…couldn't go. Ride fell through…can't bike home in the dark. But… can't go now. All red and blotchy…can't go like this." She kept sobbing and hiccupping.

"I'll go," said Marlin. "I'll go and tell him you got sick and couldn't come and sent me to tell him."

"Okay," sobbed Fiona. "Thanks."

"But come out of there, you're scaring Charlie and Nat," said Marlin.

"I don't want to," sobbed Fiona. "I just want to sit in the bathtub and wait for eternity to claim me. Just leave me alone."

The sisters tiptoed downstairs.

"She's okay," said Marlin. "She's not really going to wait for eternity to claim her, whatever that means. Listen, you two, I'm going to bike to the school. I'll be about an hour. It will still be light when I come back. Don't worry. Just watch TV or something."

Charlie and Natasha both looked frightened. No one had seen Fiona completely lose control like this before. She had been their rock through their parents' deaths and the arrival of Mrs. Weatherspoon and the move to Pine Island

and discovering the death of their great-aunt. Without her as the rock, their lives suddenly felt very shaky indeed.

Marlin settled Natasha and Charlie on the couch with a box of crackers and got on the bike, pedaling as fast as she could to the school. But by the time she got there, there was no one in front of the school or even arriving for the dance anymore. She made her way through the school's front door and to the gym.

"Wait a second, dear, what are you doing here?" asked one of the teachers who was sitting in a chair outside the gym doors. "I don't seem to recognize you."

"No, I'm Fiona McCready's sister. I just have to find this boy, Davy Clement," she said. "My sister was supposed to meet him but now she can't come."

"Okay, dear, let's go see if someone knows where he is," said the teacher, and the two of them went into the dark gym. But the teacher who knew who Davy Clement was couldn't spot him and after asking around they finally found a girl who said he had been outside the front door for a while and finally left.

"Did he go home?" Marlin tried to shout over the din of the music and talking.

"Dunno," the girl answered, shrugging. "But I haven't seen him in the gym."

"Okay, thanks," Marlin mouthed to both the girl and the teacher, and left.

By the time Marlin had biked home, Fiona had calmed down and was sitting on the couch with Charlie and Natasha looking all blotchy with puffy eyes from crying.

"It's a good thing you didn't bike to the gym yourself," said Marlin. "You look like Miss Piggy."

"Thanks," said Fiona. "What did he say?"

"He wasn't there, Fi," said Marlin. "Someone saw him waiting out front for a while and then he left. Can't you call him?"

"No, he doesn't have his own phone and he doesn't want his family to know about us. I don't even have his family's phone number. He probably hates me now anyway."

"You can't explain on Monday either because school's out," pointed out Natasha.

"Thanks for belaboring the obvious, Nat," said Marlin.

"Oh, leave her alone," said Fiona wearily. "Nothing good ever happens to this family anyway. I shouldn't have expected it."

This shocked the sisters, coming from relentlessly positive Fiona.

"Some good things happen," said Charlie. "Marlin is getting her book published."

Marlin looked at the floor. "Yeah, maybe," she muttered.

"Never mind, pass the crackers," said Fiona, and shoved a handful of them mindlessly into her mouth. She'd been too excited to do more than pick at dinner and now suddenly she was ravenous. "What's on television?"

"You choose," said Marlin.

So Fiona flipped channels until she found something she could sit through but she couldn't pay attention to the show. Her mind scurried like a rat in a wheel trying to think how she could possibly explain to Davy, if she ever saw him again, why she had stood him up. She couldn't tell him her guardian had been passed out drunk. And anything else she could think of sounded so fake and feeble. She didn't want to think about it. She would just add it to the long list of things she never wanted to think about.

She was relieved when at last they all went to bed.

She and Marlin lay looking at the Big Dipper not speaking. She knew Marlin didn't want to force her to talk if she didn't want to and she didn't much want to but she finally said, "I'm never talking to Al again."

"Fair enough," said Marlin. "I wouldn't either. From now on I'll take his dinners over myself and you can just cut him out of your life."

"Thanks," mumbled Fiona sleepily. "Were there any girls dancing in pants?"

"I didn't see any," said Marlin, trying to remember. "But it was dark."

"Oh well," said Fiona, falling asleep. "It doesn't matter now."

The Boat

MARLIN had her own reasons for wanting to take Al his dinners. That week she had received a rejection slip from Random House. When she appeared on his doorstep with his dinner he, instead of opening it and shouting "WHAT!" said quietly, "Listen, about last night—"

"Never mind about that," she said curtly. After all, how could he possibly explain himself? "I just wanted to tell you that you were right. I got a rejection slip from Random House."

"Huh," he said. "Well, that's too bad, kid. What did the family say?"

"I'm not telling them," she said. "It's too embarrassing."

He just nodded.

"But that's neither here nor there," she went on rapidly. "I still think it's a really good book and I want you to help me get it published."

"*ME?*"

"Yeah, who else do I know with a published book?"

"International bestseller," corrected Al.

"That just means a bestseller in the USA and Canada, right? I mean, it doesn't mean it's a bestseller all over the *world*," said Marlin, who since her rejection was spending more time reading about publishing in general. "Just two countries is international."

"Maybe but it so happens it *was* published all over the word, smarty-pants," said Al. "And what do you mean *just*? Do you know how many copies you have to sell to get on the bestseller list in the USA?"

"All right, and anyhow you've made my point. You're the person to help me. I want you to send it to your agent."

"Whoa, whoa."

"You still have an agent, don't you?"

"Yes, but I haven't published anything in years. And I'm not sending my agent anything I haven't even read."

"You can read it."

"What makes you think I want to?"

"I think you owe us this after what you did to Fiona. She locked herself in the bathroom and said she was going to sit in the tub and wait for eternity to claim her."

Al burst into laughter at this. "That's what she said? Wait for eternity to claim her?"

"It's not funny. She didn't even get to tell Davy why she didn't come and now school is out and she won't see him until the fall. You ruined everything for her."

Al stopped laughing abruptly. "And anyhow what

do you mean I *owe* you? Who just gave you a two-thousand-dollar engagement ring?"

"Thank you. I meant to thank you for that but there was so much going on that night. Anyhow, it doesn't change what you did to Fiona. She cried all night."

"She did, did she?" said Al, looking soberly off toward the woods. "Yeah, I guess I should come over and apologize. I really didn't mean to mess that up for her that way. I fell asleep and just kind of forgot."

"We heard. We heard *all* about it," said Marlin meaningly. "But I wouldn't come over if I were you. She's still pretty sore. She said she never wanted to see you again."

"She did, huh?" said Al.

"And Charlie doesn't want to go to look for Billy Bear with you anymore either. Because she's mad that you made Fiona cry."

"Oh, jeez."

"So, will you help me? My cookbook's on the MacBook Air but I can't lend it to you to read because I still need it to work on my second book and the others use it for the internet so I'll have to stay with you while you read it. Besides, I want to point out parts that I think I need help reworking."

"I have to read it with you staring over my shoulder? Great. Oh, all right. Bring it over. But not tonight."

"Tomorrow night when I bring dinner?"

"Not at night. I want to read it when I'm fresh. Bring it in the morning. You've got no school now, right?"

"Right."

"So bring it then," he said, and closed the door.

⟿

Al was more help than Marlin expected. He taught her how to rewrite her sentences and structure the cookbook in a more reader-friendly way.

"You know, it's not a bad cookbook," he said. "It's got, as you yourself pointed out at dinner that night, a clever title. But I know nothing about the cookbook market and publishing anything is a dicey business."

"Apparently," said Marlin dryly.

After that they worked on it every morning. Fiona had found a summer job babysitting a toddler in town so Marlin was watching over Charlie and Natasha all summer. Charlie and Natasha didn't question why Marlin went over to the trailer every morning. They were busy with their own summer pursuits. Natasha was cataloguing birds and wildlife and Charlie had Ashley over almost every day. When Ashley's mom dropped Ashley off the first morning, Marlin told Ashley's mom that she was babysitting her sisters that summer and Ashley's mom seemed to take it for granted that this was because the girls' guardian worked. Marlin said that she could babysit Ashley too if Ashley's mom could do the drop-off and pickup and Ashley's mother seemed delighted. And once when Ashley's mom couldn't pick her up, Al even agreed to drive Ashley home, bringing his truck over and pretending to have gotten home from work early.

"Delighted for free babysitting, yeah," said Fiona as the four sisters lounged around the table after dinner one night.

"Well, it's win-win," said Marlin. "Charlie likes it, don't you, Charlie? And when I'm at Al's for an hour in the morning I just make them play inside while I'm gone."

"What do you go over there for anyway?" asked Fiona.

"He's helping me with my cookbook."

"I don't know how you can stand going over. The place is such a mess."

"He actually hauled the stuff like the tub and the fridge off the front lawn and took them to the dump. And he fixed the trailer steps and window screen and took all the beer cans to recycling."

"Humph," said Fiona. "There's always more where those came from."

"There don't seem to be," said Marlin, as if realizing this for the first time. "There's a bunch of Coke cans, though. But he actually puts the empties in his recycling bin. It's a lot neater. Anyhow, we hardly notice our surroundings. Rewriting takes a lot of concentration."

"It's got nothing on babysitting a toddler," said Fiona.

Fiona had dubbed the toddler the golden beast. She

had her from nine to five every day. She would bike home every night at five-thirty done in and cranky. "There is nothing worse than spending the day trying to amuse a toddler. It's the opposite of concentration. Your mind goes to jelly. At least she takes a nap and I get one hour to read in the afternoon. Otherwise I'd go stark, staring mad."

"And at least you make a bunch of money," said Natasha. "Does that mean I get to go to strings?"

"No, Nat, I'm sorry," said Fiona. "I wasn't counting on Miss Webster and Mr. Pettinger paying for us but I kind of was counting a bit on their help with living expenses if they lived here too. Now we're back to square one and we need every penny."

"Oh, speaking of which, here." Marlin ran to her backpack and took out a stack of twenties, including the one that Fiona had given her that morning. "I was giving Al his weekly twenty bucks and he not only gave it back, he gave back *all* the twenties we gave him."

Fiona took the pile of twenties and stared at them as if she didn't know what they were.

"Well, there's a surprise," she said finally.

"He said to make sure Charlie knew and that also, Charlie, you know that you are still welcome to come look for Billy Bear with him every Saturday if you want. He says he's still going."

Charlie shook her head.

"Go if you want," said Fiona. "Don't mind me."

"And he also said that he's going to come over and talk to you after dinner tonight, Fiona. He has a plan."

"Oh, gee, what now?" said Fiona. "Didn't he get the message that I don't want to see him?"

"He's very sorry about, you know, what happened," said Marlin.

"I still don't want to talk to him. Not ever," said Fiona.

"Well, you don't have to," said Marlin. "But you know what Mom used to say about forgiving your enemies."

"Not ever," repeated Fiona. "Besides, I have bigger things to worry about."

"What?" asked Marlin.

"Oh, just the usual," said Fiona, sighing and putting her dishes in the sink. Because she was babysitting all day, they apportioned the chores so that Charlie and Natasha did the dishes and Marlin cooked dinner as she always had and made the lunches. "I'm going to go take a bath."

Fiona lay in the bath worrying. Mr. Pennypacker, after a period of quiet, had taken to writing increasingly threatening subject lines on his emails. MUST READ!!! TIME-SENSITIVE!!! WILL HAVE TO CONTACT SOCIAL SERVICES IF SILENCE CONTINUES!!! It was this last that worried her the most. She had told him that Al had misplaced the paperwork regarding Martha's wish to have Al as the legal guardian but promised him that she would update him as soon as possible. But that was when she thought they would be adopted and the problem was soon to be solved if she could just put him off with a little lie. Now she didn't know what to do. Every day she expected to come home to find a social worker sitting on the front porch or maybe even a police officer. Was it a crime to lie to everyone and stay in Canada without legal status or a guardian? Probably. They could be deported, she supposed. They weren't Canadians, they were American citizens by birth. Round and round her head went these thoughts, driving her crazy, keeping her up at night. She was so worried she forgot what Marlin had said about Al coming over until there was a knock on the door.

She leapt out of the tub but she could hear Marlin downstairs handling it.

"No," she heard her say. "She doesn't want to talk to you. Charlie is hiding in her room. She doesn't want to talk to you either."

"Listen, I only came over partly because of that. I think we may have a nibble for your book. My agent doesn't handle cookbooks but he liked the idea so he sent a query to a friend of his who does. She's a good agent, she handles cookbooks, and she wants to see it."

"She wants to see my book!" shrieked Marlin.

"So, come on, come over to the trailer and let's put together a smoking letter to go with the manuscript."

"FIONA!" shouted Marlin. "I'm going to Al's!"

"Fine!" shouted Fiona from the bathroom.

"Hi, Fiona!" shouted Al. "I know you don't want to hear it, but I'm very sorry about my oversight."

Fiona didn't answer. *Oversight?* For a word person he had picked a very inadequate one. Or maybe that's how he was writing off the whole incident to salve his conscience.

"And I have a plan about that if you want to hear it!" Al continued.

Fiona stayed quiet.

"I thought I'd drive you over to Davy Clement's house and you could just tell him what happened. You know, that I fell asleep and couldn't take you. Just explain."

"Are you nuts?" shouted Fiona.

"What? It wasn't *your* fault."

"I don't know where he lives!"

"I do. I looked it up."

"His family doesn't know about us. What would they *think*?" shouted Fiona.

"Well, then write him a note. I've got the address for you although you could have found that yourself with a little digging."

"Go away!" shouted Fiona. "This is none of your business and I don't want to talk to you."

"McCready women," Fiona could hear him saying to Marlin. "Hard nuts to crack."

When Marlin finished at Al's and had returned home and gone to bed, she turned to Fiona and said, "You know Random House rejected my book."

"Did they?" said Fiona tactfully because she had guessed this before from the way Marlin had changed the subject whenever anyone brought it up.

"But if Al can help me get it published and if I could get the advance money this summer, you could stop babysitting."

"That would be nice," said Fiona wearily, and rolled over to fall asleep.

But all the next day it was at the back of Fiona's mind. That dangerous little gleam of hope. If one of them were to pull off some kind of spectacular coup, it would be Marlin. She was the most original of the four of them. The one most prone to thinking outside the box. It would be like her to save them by becoming a bestselling author. Fiona's mind went to new clothes and no worry about bills and maybe even college educations. She was practical enough to know that it was unlikely Marlin would ever get published let alone make a lot of money from it but it gave her a pleasant day's daydreaming while she pushed the golden beast in her swing and filled the void where her daydreaming about Davy had been.

All the way home as she pedaled along she elaborated on this daydream. Now the four of them were going to Europe together on vacations when Marlin became the first person to win the Nobel Prize for Literature for a cookbook and like *Martha's Boat,* it became an international bestseller. She was having a wonderful time embroidering this fantasy but when she pulled the bike into the front yard her heart dropped. Sitting on the front porch was a woman in a good pants suit chatting away to Charlie.

Social services, thought Fiona. This was a social worker if ever she'd seen one. She'd come when Fiona wasn't even there to handle the situation. And if the social worker had to chat with someone did it have to be Charlie? Charlie, who, despite her best intentions, always gave everything away. And there was Charlie, true to form, nattering away, bright-eyed and bushy-tailed and no doubt ruining everything.

The woman stood up when she saw Fiona and said, "Oh my, you must be Charlie's big sister, Fiona. She has told me so much about you."

Oh no, oh no, thought Fiona. What had Charlie said? Whatever it was she could see all her hard work going for nothing. This was it. It was all over. They would be split up and scattered to the winds and there wasn't a thing she could do about it.

"Yes, I'm Fiona." She was suddenly unable to speak above a whisper.

"I'm Mrs. Masterson. I work for social services," said the woman.

"Who sent you?" croaked Fiona. "Mr. Pennypacker?"

"No, it was Charlie's friend Ashley's mother. She was concerned about something Charlie had said to Ashley. So, I just thought I would toodle over and have a little look-see."

Oh no, thought Fiona. *Charlie, what have you done to us?*

"But fortunately," Mrs. Masterson went on, "Mr. Farber has explained it all. How the trailer next door is his office. And especially about the paperwork getting lost when your aunt unexpectedly died. My, what a lot of troubles you girls have seen! Thank goodness for Mr. Farber, as I'm sure you all say to yourselves daily."

"Oh," said Fiona, sitting rapidly down with weak knees onto a porch chair.

At that moment Al, Marlin, and Natasha came out carrying glasses of lemonade. Al had on a clean polo shirt and a pair of chinos. He was freshly shaved and smelled of soap. He smiled at both Fiona and Mrs. Masterson, oozing charm from every pore, and said, "Well, well, well, I see you've met our little Fiona. Have a lemonade, Fiona, you're looking a mite peaked."

"Here, take mine," said Natasha, handing hers to Fiona and disappearing back into the house.

To hide, thought Fiona enviously.

"Fiona babysits in town for pocket money," Al went on in syrupy tones. "Quite the entrepreneur, our Fiona."

"How lovely, dear. That was my summer job when I was your age as well."

"Was it?" said Al smoothly, handing Mrs. Masterson a glass. "There you go, Fiona. Play your cards right and you too can grow up to be a social worker."

Fiona smiled dully. She knew Mrs. Masterson had no idea how mocking Al was being. His whole appearance and manner were courtly to the point of playacting.

"When I talked to your sister Marlin this morning," said Mrs. Masterson, "she said Mr. Farber would explain everything when he got home from the store. Then he called and even invited me out to see the farm. It's a long drive from Shoreline but I just love St. Mary's By the Sea. So picturesque. And this farm! Beautiful old acreage and heritage buildings."

"Oh," said Fiona.

"Now, I'd love to stay and chat with all of you some more but I've had two glasses of this terrific lemonade that I hear is Marlin's original recipe and I really do have to scoot. We're dreadfully understaffed. Just stop in with the paperwork, Mr. Farber, next time you're in Shoreline. No rush. At your leisure when you dig it up."

"Will do," said Al. "And please call me Al."

Mrs. Masterson simpered. Marlin rolled her eyes and Fiona shot her a warning glance.

"We're so happy you could visit. Let me see you to your car," Al went on as he walked her down the driveway to where she was parked.

"Charlie, what did Mrs. Masterson mean that she was here because of something you said?" hissed Fiona when Mrs. Masterson was out of earshot.

"Nothing!" said Charlie.

"Mrs. Masterson said that Ashley told her mom that Charlie's favorite game with the dolls was let's pretend the parents are dead and the children are secretly living alone," said Marlin.

"Argh," groaned Fiona despairingly. "We were so busy keeping adults at bay it never occurred to me that Charlie's doll would give it away. But Ashley's dad must have seen Al at our house during the search for Natasha. And Al drove Ashley home that time."

"Yeah, but Ashley told her that she always saw Al's truck parked next door at the trailer and after Ashley told her about the doll game, Ashley's mom began to connect the two things and wonder because Al's truck *shouldn't* have been at the trailer next door when he was supposed to be at *work* all day. So she called social services and Mrs. Masterson called here and got me," Marlin went on, "and

I called Al and Al called Mrs. Masterson back and he invited her to come over and he met her here, all cleaned up, and we all pretended that he was the guardian. He even shaved his beard to make a better impression. And he explained the trailer was his office and sometimes he drove there even though it was just next door and Mrs. Masterson believed him because I think by the time he was done with her she was half in love with him."

They watched Al as his conversation with Mrs. Masterson ended and he slapped the hood of her car and she drove off waving gaily out the window. Then he headed back and came onto the porch.

"Well, that went well," he said smugly.

"Yeah, thanks," said Fiona.

"No more than I contracted for," said Al. "Except, of course, I gave you that money back so I guess you do owe me. A simple thanks will do."

"I said thanks," said Fiona coldly.

"Listen, Fiona, how long are you going to stay mad at me?" asked Al.

"I'm not mad at you, I'm completely indifferent," said Fiona. "I appreciate what you did for us but it's only stop-gap measures. She's going to want to see paperwork we don't have and I don't have a solution for that."

Al rubbed his chin. "No, I guess not," he murmured.

"And you may have given the money back but you're still getting meals, aren't you?" said Fiona, and flounced into the house.

"Speaking of which," said Al, "why don't I take my supper now and save you a trip, Marl."

"She's Marlin to you!" called Fiona from inside. "I'm the only one allowed to call her Marl."

"Listen, don't push my patience!" called Al back.

"I can push anything I want. You're not my *real* guardian!" shouted Fiona.

"Yeah and you'd better hope Mrs. Masterson doesn't find that out!" shouted Al back angrily.

"Don't yell at Fiona!" said Charlie, who had been watching this whole exchange worriedly.

"Oh, Charlie, give me a break, will you?" snapped Al, and left before Marlin could get his dinner into a food container.

Marlin had sent the manuscript out to the agent just that afternoon so Marlin no longer worked with Al in the morning and he wasn't answering Marlin's knocks at dinnertime but only leaving his empty food container outside the front door with a note saying Marlin should leave the dinner there and not disturb him, he was busy.

When a week went by and Al brought no news from the agent, Marlin decided to get back to work writing the second book in the series.

Midsummer came and Fiona began to relax because she had stopped once again getting threatening emails from Mr. Pennypacker and she hadn't heard any more from Mrs. Masterson. Maybe Mrs. Masterson had forgotten them! Or the paperwork. Al had been cleaned up and convincing as their guardian. Perhaps if social services was so busy and understaffed the McCreadys weren't worth their bother.

Just when Fiona began to relax about this she biked into the yard one night after a particularly difficult day with the golden beast, who had been in a bad mood and crying most of the day, to find not Al, not Mrs. Masterson, but Mr. Pennypacker sitting on the porch. He was still in his tie and vest so she guessed he had come straight from the office. He looked official and frightening and less like a garden gnome than the angel of death.

He didn't even greet her as she climbed the steps. They simply looked at each other silently. She the elusive victim of his emails and he the phantom of dread.

"So," she said finally, and sat down.

"Yes, you really have behaved unforgivably. I don't often have to chase clients down to their houses."

"I don't suppose you often have clients with as much to lose," said Fiona tiredly.

"Or to gain. That's what's so aggravating. I'm a busy man and I'm taking time to drive all the way out here to give you news that is beneficial to you because you refuse to answer my emails and as we know you are equally bad about Canada Post and phone calls. I'd half a mind to let the whole thing drop and let you lose the boat sale but I couldn't do that to Martha. It was in her memory that I finally came before the potential buyer found something else."

"Boat sale?" said Fiona.

"I see you not only didn't answer them, you didn't even read my emails. Yes, as you know, I said I would handle the sale for you and there is a couple anxious to buy and I have negotiated a very good price. But as the owner you need to approve the deal and sign the paperwork."

"Oh my gosh!" said Fiona, relief flooding her. "I'm so sorry. I thought, I thought it was bad news."

"No, very good news indeed," said Mr. Pennypacker primly.

He passed the sales contract to her and she nearly fainted when she saw the figure. This was another year's survival for them!

"Read it through before you sign," he warned.

"I don't have to," said Fiona. "We need the money."

"Yes, I'd say you do," said Mr. Pennypacker.

When she'd signed it, he sighed. "I'm going to waive my fee as well. There was not a lot that Martha would let me do for her during her life and I take satisfaction in being able to look after her estate for you, as I believe she might have been grateful for, if she knew. And the boat, well, it gives me a turn, frankly, to see it sold. That boat was everything to Martha. Seeing it go is, well, like seeing the last of her go. I cannot view it purely as a business transaction, you understand. What it is to you, a source of revenue, is not what it is to me. Nor for that matter what it was to her."

"Yes," said Fiona. "Martha's boat. Al's book. He says in the book that she loved her boat and wouldn't marry him because of fishing. Because she preferred that life to him. That she loved it more than him."

"Well, perhaps," said Mr. Pennypacker. "She certainly loved it more than she did either of us. I like to think she didn't love Al Farber and anyhow had better taste than to marry a wastrel like him. I like to think if she were to accept anyone's proposal it would have been mine but she didn't. She wasn't interested in marrying anyone. She said everyone needs two things in life—a family and a purpose—and her boat was those two things to her and she needed nothing else. So it seems strange to think of her boat being sold. It was . . . so much her. Her family *and* her purpose. Well, I mustn't be sentimental. *Omnia temporaria sunt* as they say."

Fiona was quiet. Mr. Pennypacker looked pained now as he held the sales contract tightly in his hands. And she realized that she had known two men who knew and loved and mourned her aunt when none of the four of them had, despite inheriting nearly everything she had owned. It must be strange for Al and Mr. Pennypacker.

"I'm sorry," she said finally. It was all she could think of to say.

"Yes, well," he said. Then he shook himself out slightly. "And there's another matter. Maybe even a more important matter as far as you're concerned. Al Farber has been in to see me. He has asked me to speak to you about a delicate matter. He did not want to speak of it himself because he is of the impression that you"—he nodded to Fiona—"were not interested in talking to him. But he feels that it's in Charlie's best interest and so he asked me to come and put the matter before you. He knows that as much as I dislike him I would also approve the arrangement. For one thing I would no longer have to try to track *you* down." He nodded at Fiona again. "Which has become a considerable pain in the neck, if you must know. And I *do* approve the arrangement, since it looks as if he has cleaned up his act as they say. Of course, I never did believe he'd been appointed your legal guardian although I was willing to cut you a great deal of slack waiting for proof. It was highly unprofessional on my part and highly uncharacteristic but all that I did concerning you I did for Martha. I tried to think what she would have wanted. I feel I have in that sense been true to her memory. I do not know what she would think but I do not think she would be displeased since he appears to be trying to move forward as an upright citizen despite, shall we say, his natural predilection. Of course, whether he can keep this up or not is unknown. And not that this plan he has come to me with is up to me. It is wholly up to the four of you."

"What?" piped up Marlin, who, with Charlie and Natasha, had been cavesdropping from the kitchen and now that they could hear that nothing terrible was going on had crept out to the porch and seated themselves next to Fiona. "Is he talking about a book contract? Is it about my book?"

"A book contract?" said Mr. Pennypacker, raising his eyebrows in surprise. "No. He wants to adopt you."

"*Adopt* us?" said Fiona in astonishment. She felt sure Mr. Pennypacker must have gotten this part wrong.

"Yes, all four of you."

They sat silently stunned. Whatever Fiona had expected it had not been this.

"Would he, would he want to *live* here?" asked Fiona, because as much as she could see this taking care of a lot of problems and allowing the four of them to stay together she did not like the idea of Al Farber stomping around the house barking "WHAT!" day and night.

"No. He says he wants you to know that he has given

up his, his, uh, beer habit and has gone back to writing but he does not wish to live in your house. However, his trailer can be moved to your property. He simply has to have some work done. A small septic field put in and some water lines run. If you are amenable to this, and to the adoption itself, he thinks it a good idea to, as he put it, get a move on before Mrs. Masterson sticks her nose in it again."

"Will he be, what will he be, our father?" asked Charlie, looking confused.

"No!" roared Fiona before she could help it.

"Well, what?" asked Natasha.

"He'll be…" Marlin thought about it. "Our very own on-site waste troll."

Another Happy Middle

MR. Pennypacker arranged for the adoption. Al moved his trailer to the property and two noisy companies came to put in a septic field and run water lines and finally he was hooked up. Then the trailer went on cement blocks.

"I guess that means you're not moving anywhere soon," said Marlin.

"Look on the bright side, neither are you," said Al.

The first Saturday he was there he took Fiona in the pickup to town to buy groceries.

"You really don't have to do this," said Fiona. "You don't have to do anything differently. I don't mind biking in."

"I wanted to talk to you anyway," said Al, looking at the road and not at her.

"Oh," said Fiona. It was still awkward between them.

"If this arrangement is going to work we're going to have to be friends," said Al.

"We are friends," said Fiona slowly. "Of a sort."

"I mean I don't want to feel like given half a chance you'd throw the kitchen knives at me."

"I don't dislike you," said Fiona. "I really appreciate what you did. And I'll try to keep everyone out of your hair. It's the least we can do. Because of you the four of us can stay together and that's all I ever wanted. I just don't understand why you're doing it."

"What do you care why I'm doing it? Now that you've got your rear end in a tub of butter?"

"Is it because of Martha? Are you doing it for *her*? Like Mr. Pennypacker waived his fee and handled her estate because he was doing it for her? I mean Mr. Pennypacker says you even gave up beer. Or is it for Charlie?"

"Listen, the beer was more of, I don't know, a bad habit. It was never a big deal for me, evidence of prom night aside."

"Summer Fling, not prom," corrected Fiona.

"Whatever. I just went on autopilot in a way after Martha rejected me. I didn't seem to have any point. I didn't know what to do with myself. My point had been her. But that's over. And now I've started writing again so I need a clear head."

"You've started writing again?"

"Yeah, well, we can't have Marlin getting on the best-seller list before I have my next book out."

"Wow. What are you writing about? Is it another biography?"

"First of all, I don't talk about my books when I'm

writing them. Secondly, no, it's a novel. And to your former question, yes, partly I am taking the four of you on because of Martha. And partly because of Charlie. And partly I don't know why. Masochism maybe. But here is the thing—you need to understand some things about this arrangement. I'm not just living on the property. I'm not just adopting you on paper. I'm doing it properly. Which means I will be picking up the bills."

"How? You don't seem much better off than we are. You live in a trailer!"

"I bought the trailer because I needed something to live in when I bought the property next to Martha's. I always thought we'd end up together and I'd move into her house and we'd join our properties. When she died, I couldn't really believe that it never happened. That it never *would* happen. It kind of threw me for a loop. Well, anyway, that's neither here nor there. The point is that I didn't live in the trailer because that's all I could afford. I thought I was living there temporarily waiting for Martha. But I've got plenty of money in the bank. You know I had an *international bestseller*, Fiona. I've got plenty of money and I'm planning on making more."

"But you took our twenties?"

"You annoyed me. With your presumption that I should just roll over and solve your problems."

"But now you are."

"I wouldn't push it."

"Well, even so, you don't have to pay our bills," said Fiona. "I can take care of that end of it."

"Bullrushes!" said Al. "You think I don't see you going around biting your nails? Don't be a martyr. If someone offers you help, take it. You can help someone else down the line if you're so proud."

"That's what Miss Webster said," said Fiona.

"Oh, the worshipped Miss Webster," said Al. "Hear from her lately? Because it looks to me like it was one Walmart bill and she was out of there."

"Stop it, she was nice," said Fiona. "She's probably pretty busy. Just married and all."

"Uh-huh," said Al. "So, anyhow, three points. First, you can quit the babysitting job now. Second, I'm picking up groceries starting today. After all, those groceries feed me too."

"Thanks. They'll have to find a replacement for me before I can quit but that would be great."

"And third point, tell Natasha she can join strings. It worries Charlie. I can pay for it. Drop in the bucket."

"Okay," said Fiona. "That's generous. Natasha can thank you herself for that one."

"The only thing I demand in return is that none of you bother me when I'm writing. If I'm going to pay for all this stuff, I have to earn a living and I can't do that if you're constantly bothering me. I don't really look forward to living with a bunch of children but if I do and if you knock on my door when I'm working, it had better be because there's blood running down someone's arms."

"I promise," said Fiona. "We all promise. I promise on their behalf."

By the end of the week the family Fiona worked for had found another babysitter and although a lot of summer was gone, Fiona settled down to enjoy what was left of it. She took to biking into town and if she happened to frequently find herself on the block with the fudge stand it was probably coincidence. But as often as she appeared there she never saw Davy Clement. Perhaps his family went away for the summer, she thought, and anyway maybe by the fall she would know what to say to him.

Fiona kept her promise faithfully not to bother Al while he was working but the other three let that rule slide as they got used to Al being around.

He had taken on a lot of little chores in the time he didn't spend writing. He installed for them a longed-for porch swing. He cleaned the gutters so the roof stopped leaking during heavy rains. He promised to help Natasha cut a pathway through the woods to the top of the mountain because she had heard that the birds of prey on Pine Island gathered there in September and took off in a series of clouds to migrate south. She had read on the internet that it was quite the sight and she thought if she had a clear pathway cut through the bush to the mountaintop she wouldn't get lost when she climbed up to watch.

Fiona was sitting on the porch swing reading one summer day and keeping an eye out so that her sisters didn't knock on the trailer door, which they tended to do if she didn't fend them off. But they had a way of finding their way there when she periodically went back into the house.

Natasha had decided the weather was cool enough for her and Al to take their cutting tools and work on the path so she knocked on his trailer door when Fiona disappeared from the porch.

"Do you want to cut the trail now?" she asked when he answered it.

"I'M WORKING!" Al roared. "I keep telling you, save it for the weekend!"

Charlie had found dozens of reasons to knock on the door that day and was never dissuaded by Al's refusals, which were never as shouty and loud as he was with the rest of them.

"Can we go to see Billy?" she asked when again Fiona had disappeared.

"I'm working," he said. "And it's not Saturday. Go away."

"Ashley couldn't come over, can you give me a lift there?" she asked an hour later.

"Not right now, I'M *WORKING*!"

The latest was, "I know we can't get a horse but what about a puppy?"

"A *DOG*?" Al roared this one, so startled was he, but Charlie was undeterred.

"We have a big fenced meadow. We could get two. So they can play together when we're at school."

"*DOGS*? You want *TWO* dogs? Oh, all right," he said as Charlie's lip began to tremble. "I guess a couple of dogs would be okay but I don't want to talk about it until after dinner. I'M WORKING!"

Marlin came to the door the most that afternoon. She had endless questions about the book she was working on, things she needed to ask him that could not wait, was this sentence better or this one? Did she need a comma here? And endless queries about when she would hear from the agent. The new agent was sending the cookbook around but so far she had met only with rejection.

"So, do you think I should give it to another agent?" asked Marlin when Al, looking a bit wild-eyed, had answered the door yet again.

"I'M WORKING!" roared Al.

"WELL, SO AM I!" roared Marlin, who always gave as good as she got.

Al was about to go inside when Marlin calmed down and said, "Do you think it's ever going to get published? EVER?"

Al stopped and looked thoughtful. "Well, you never know about the vagaries of publishing houses but I'd say it has a shot. It seems like a good book to me. Nothing out there quite like it as far as I can see."

"Yeah, but are you just saying that to make me feel better?"

"Marlin," said Al with increasing impatience, "you may not be able to count on me for much but you can *depend* on me to tell you the truth. Who told you earlier that sending it in over the transom to Random House was going to get you nowhere when everyone else just wanted to make you feel good by saying the book would be published. *WHO?*"

"You," said Marlin in a small voice.

"Well then!" barked Al, and slammed the door in her face.

Fiona smiled as she returned to the porch and witnessed this transaction. Al's shouting and blustering no longer bothered her. How had it happened, she wondered, that in the few months they had lived on Pine Island he had become part of them? His quirks and qualities had blended in with their own so that shouting "WHAT!" was part of the makeup of their entity. The one they were all together. She still believed she could save them through the force of her determination. Charlie still always had one eye out for danger. Natasha still floated through life alive in the moment without any thought to what might happen next and Marlin's feet were still planted firmly on the ground but now they had Al, who blustered and roared but always told the truth, no matter how painful. And like all their qualities, good and bad, Fiona would not change his now that he was part of them. She would not know who she was, before without the three of them, but now without the four.

"Fiona!" roared Al from the trailer steps. "I've had so many interruptions I need to work through dinner. I'll need supper in the trailer."

"Yes, sir, right away, sir," muttered Fiona.

She sighed and put down her book. Sometimes Al joined them for dinner but more often he chose to have it in the trailer as he worked. She could hear Marlin checking things in the oven and she went inside to put Al's supper in a food container. By the time she got it out to him he was back inside typing at his computer. He answered the door looking half crazed and handed her the empty, dirty food container from the night before.

"You know," said Fiona, "the least you could do, if we're taking you your dinner, is to wash out the food container before returning it."

"The *LEAST* I can do?" he roared. "The *least*? Who is cutting trails through the woods, rewriting cookbooks, paying bills, dealing with that garden gnome night and day, apparently now buying *DOGS*, writing, for God's sake, another book through endless interruptions so that maybe *SOMEONE* might have a college education. I'm the guy doing all those things for you, when *WHAT* for Christ's sake do you imagine *you* are to *ME*?" And he slammed back into his trailer before she could reply.

Fiona stared at the empty trailer steps where Al had been. She thought of the Big Dipper making its transit every night across their bedroom window. Shining brilliantly as if just for her and Marlin and disappearing. The terrible sadness of people she loved doing the same. The frightening knowledge that people you were part of could be just *gone*. The hope that all of them would one day appear again as the Dipper did each night but how you just didn't *know*. She guessed it was this way for everyone. Al had lost Billy and Martha but for now he had the four sisters. She smiled suddenly because she knew who they were to him. Who everyone is to each other. "We're your boat."

Acknowledgments

Many thanks to Andrea Cascardi, Margaret Ferguson, Lynne Missen, and Ken Setterington.